CATHERINE GRANT

VENTURE INTO DESTINY

Complete and Unabridged

LINFORD
Leicester

First published in Great Britain in 1976 by
Robert Hale Limited
London

First Linford Edition
published 2010
by arrangement with
Robert Hale Limited
London

British Library CIP Data

Grant, Catherine.
  Venture into destiny.- -
  (Linford romance library)
  1. Love stories.
  2. Large type books.
  I. Title II. Series
  823.9'14–dc22

  ISBN 978–1–44480–035–7

Published by
F. A. Thorpe (Publishing)
Anstey, Leicestershire

Set by Words & Graphics Ltd.
Anstey, Leicestershire
Printed and bound in Great Britain by
T. J. International Ltd., Padstow, Cornwall

This book is printed on acid-free paper

1

'Oh do hurry up Anne. We'll never catch that train if you dawdle at this rate,' complained Melanie.

'Now look here, my girl, I certainly can't help it if I'm half asleep until at least noon every day.'

Melanie silently shook her head. After sharing this flat with Anne for the last four years she would have thought that Anne's dilatory ways would produce no effect on her at all; still she was the one to worry and harass when things were not going right. This fine June morning they were setting off from Durham to attend a clerical course at York; it was being organised from the office where they both worked. They were quite looking forward to the change, as lately, the tedium of office life was becoming increasingly abhorrent to the girls.

She sighed audibly and scanned the headlines in the morning paper whilst waiting for Anne to announce she was ready. It was no good; she couldn't concentrate on the newsprint. Melanie looked around her, admiring their small pieces of junk they had collected for the past four years. Melanie thought how lucky they had been to get this flat and remembered the first day they had met.

She had been working in the government offices for two years before Anne had joined the staff in the same department. They had taken an instant liking to each other. Anne admitted that previously she had tried a nursing career but had found that she just wasn't cut out for that particular vocation. Melanie explained that she lived in a furnished bedsitter on the outskirts of the city. Her parents were killed in a road accident ten years ago, she was only ten then and had gone to live with an aunt until she was seventeen. Then she had moved out of an already overcrowded household as her aunt had four children of her own, all younger than Melanie. She liked her independence, still visited her aunt and family regularly, but would prefer a flat instead of the bedsitter eventually.

Anne related how unbearable things were at home for herself. Her mother had been a widow for several years and married again two years ago. She just could not get on with her stepfather although he always behaved nicely to her when her mother was present.

'I think that's why I went in for nursing. It would mean that I lived in a hostel while training for the job and so I didn't have to go home very often,' reflected Anne. At the present she was living at home until she found a suitable place for herself. They both agreed to share a flat and started searching for one straight away.

After two weeks, they found a suitable place, situated in an old narrow street quite near the magnificent cathedral and the rent was not too exhorbitant. It consisted of three rooms, sitting room, one large bedroom and a tiny kitchen. The bathroom was shared with the rest of the tenants in this large terraced house. Although it was furnished, there were just the bare essentials: namely, twin beds and an enormous wardrobe with matching tallboy, a large lumpy sofa of indeterminate age, table and chairs, and in the kitchen an assortment of cupboards with an historic looking gas cooker. Over the past four years they had added little touches here and there to brighten the place up. Gay cotton curtains, bright shaggy rugs, their own personalities were reflected by way of pen and ink drawings on the walls from Melanie and Anne's flair for decorating had proved very enterprising in its bright and modern decor.

Her thoughts flew back to the present as she realised that Anne was hovering in the doorway, case in hand, waiting for her.

'Now who's doing the dawdling? Come on, we're walking to the station, you know, not taxi-ing. So get a move on.'

Melanie hastily gathered her case and bag and with a last look round the room turned and left.

Half an hour later with what seemed only seconds to spare, they had reached the station and were boarding the train for York. Both Melanie and Anne were small in height and slim, although there the similarities ended because to Melanie's olive skin and green eyes, Anne had a fair complexion and grey eyes. Melanie decided to travel in her bright green demi skirt with a paler green swing jacket. Her midnight dark hair she had coiled around the crown of her head and the style added a little height to her stature. Anne, slightly less conventional, was dressed in her faded blue levis with an even more faded blue denim shirt. Her fair hair was swinging loosely to her shoulders and they both looked equally attractive in their own styles.

At York, their first destination was to

register at the hotel allocated to them for the duration of the course. It was a charming old fashioned coaching inn. Melanie considered their shared room as charming as the public rooms below; the smell of beeswax polish was everywhere, with low ceilings and historic atmosphere pervading along the hushed corridors.

'One good thing about working at a government office, they don't stint themselves about your expenses,' drawled Anne as she was unpacking.

'Don't you believe it, dear, you should have seen old Arthur's face when I asked for an advance for us for our rail fares. Honestly he looked at me as if I had made an improper suggestion.'

The official cordially welcomed them at the York office and proceeded to show them around the various departments. When he took them into the Finance section they were afire with questions to the three girls and only one man working there. This was due to the fact that they worked in the corresponding department back home. Mr Sykes then left them to take notes and compare work routines. Melanie observed that Anne seemed more impressed with the young man called Robert and that he seemed to reciprocate the feeling too.

That evening whilst having dinner at the hotel, Melanie noticed Anne was unusually quiet but did not comment on it. However in the bar, later out of concern for her friend's silence she asked her the reason.

'Nothing . . . well er . . . ' then looking past Melanie with an expression of panic on her face, she continued in a rush of words, 'You know Robert . . . he's invited himself over for a drink tonight and guess what, he's here now . . . hello Robert, nice of you to come.'

Melanie smiled to herself as she turned to greet the young man; honestly, Anne was the limit.

'Hi there girls. What are you both drinking?' said a cheerful male voice. As he sauntered off to the bar, Anne, red-faced, apologized to her friend for not telling her earlier. She didn't want to leave Melanie on her own tonight but in her own words 'Robert had bowled her over' and she wanted to make the most of her one and only night here, in cementing their budding friendship.

Robert returned from the bar with his tray of drinks and Melanie thought he looked very attractive. Tall, brown haired, fairly longish with red glints in it as the bar lights shone on his hair; Melanie did not blame her flatmate for pursuing the friendship.

'Can I show you girls the city tonight?' asked Robert after he had settled comfortably beside Anne, his drink in front of him.

Melanie told them both emphatically to 'count her out' of the evening's entertainment. She was going into the residents' lounge later to make some final notes to her work of the day, whilst her memory was still fresh. They made half hearted attempts to dissuade her but Melanie was adamant; and presently, after they had finished their drinks, Anne and Robert said their goodnights and left the hotel.

She had no intentions of doing any further work, it had only been an excuse of course, and instead of leaving, ordered another vodka. There were not many people there, as she looked around the bar; two young couples, the bartender, two young men who looked like firm representatives drinking and arguing amicably together and herself completed the occupants. And then, as is usually the case when sitting in a bar, her attention was caught by the entrance of a new customer about to pass near her on the way to order a drink.

Jake paused in the bar entrance to let his eyes become accustomed to the gloom of the dimly lit room after his stroll outside in the evening sunshine. He felt much better now after his hour's exercise, for he had been driving for hours that day, travelling up from the south coast. His long limbs felt a little looser and his brain less tired. He looked casually round the bar and caught a young girl in the act of staring at him openly. Rather attractive piece of the opposite sex, he thought to himself, although a bit obvious with that stare. He, in turn, stared openly back at her, admiring the curves of her slim figure through the pretty cream maxi dress she was wearing.

Melanie looked hastily away as she realized that the fascinating stranger had noticed her appraisal. She could feel her face slowly reddening at the thoughts of this stranger misconstruing her interest. But he was worth a second glance from any woman. He was well over six feet in height, broad, powerful shoulders clad casually in blue open-necked denim shirt, tucked in well fitting denim jeans. For all his informal attire his very air was one of masculine elegance. The man's face was devastatingly attractive, tanned a deep bronze that could not have been obtained anywhere in this country, and darkish hair which was long and thick, ending at his shirt collar. But his scar which ran from his forehead to his right eyebrow added rather than detracted from his rugged, handsome appearance. She judged him to be in his late thirties as he bought his drink and walked over to a seat by the window, directly opposite herself, yet the width of the room was between them.

Melanie had been so absorbed in scrutinizing the man that she had not noticed one of the young men who had been standing at the bar come over to her.

'I've noticed you sitting all by yourself since your friends left you. Ken Waites is my name and I'd very much like to buy you a drink.'

'I'm sorry but . . .'

'Okay . . . I know this introduction doesn't look too good but I'm sure you're a stranger here like myself. What's wrong with a couple of drinks to pass away the time?'

His voice was soft and boyish, like the sheepish grin he flashed at her and so she couldn't resist a small smile in return. As he moved over to the bar to replenish their glasses she unwittingly looked over to find the man with the scar watching intently. Their eyes met as he raised his glass to his lips, hers startled, his distinctly mocking. Who on earth did he think he was? God's gift to women? However, his scornful glance did make her slightly uncomfortable.

An hour later she felt even more uncomfortable and not a little angry with herself. Why on earth had she let this creep pick her up; she had been bored to tears within ten minutes of meeting him. Ken was drinking gins as if it was going out of fashion; it must be obvious to all in the bar that he had drunk one too many. She tried to excuse herself earlier and retreat to her room but his loud verbal protest, which had caused several heads to turn in their direction, had quickly put an end

12

to her escape. On and on he talked, about his fantastic job and super job prospects. He certainly had a clever impression of himself, his speech began to slur and his face more and more flushed with the alcohol and his heady speech.

'Say, this bar's getting crowded . . . lesh take a bottle to my room.'

Melanie was absolutely staggered by his suggestion and could feel the bottled up anger starting to erupt in her. She was way out of her depth with this character and as she started to frame her angry retorts to him she saw his bleary gaze transfer from her face to something behind her.

'I think the young . . . er . . . lady has had enough of your company tonight. I suggest you collect your key at the desk and enjoy a good night's sleep.' His voice was deep, as she knew it would be, with a hint of a Northern drawl in it. However he looked at Melanie contemptuously. She sat transfixed at the whole scene, unable to move or utter a word. Ken started to make a protest and then, noticing the determined look in the stranger's eyes and also the powerful stature of the man, with his authorative air, decided to give up the mental struggle. He muttered his goodnights and tried to walk as jauntily as possible out of the room.

They watched him leave, the silence stretching between Melanie and the man. She had stood up to go and he had not moved away from her, he was so close she could smell his tangy aftershave and a spicy, clean scent from him. His eyes were a cold, steely grey and as she stared straight at him she could almost feel the strange animal magnetism from him. The thoughts made her shiver and it broke the stillness between them.

'Thanks for your help,' she stammered, but he cut in abruptly, 'I was passing on my way out and couldn't help but overhear his suggestion to you. I realized you were outraged but, honey . . . you asked for it all, didn't you?

After all, even I got the 'come on' from you when I came in tonight.' With these last searing words he turned his back on her and disappeared out of the door leading to the street outside.

Her face was scarlet with mortification, she collected her key and hastily made her way to her room. She knew there was an element of truth in what he had said and felt her skin crawl with shame at his cutting words. When Anne returned from her date a few minutes later Melanie was preparing for bed.

'What a marvellous night, Melanie. We're going to write to each other . . . oh, and Rob's seeing us both off at the station tomorrow night.' On and on her friend chattered, but Melanie nodded in the right places, her mind was elsewhere and wishing that they were indeed standing at that station tomorrow. She decided not to mention the incident to Anne, it would mar her friend's delightful evening. As she drifted off to sleep she remembered a deep, husky voice, and his face was clearly etched in her memory.

Two weeks later, they were returning home from a day's work. Melanie was driving 'Hercules', as her car was fondly christened. It was an old Morris and she had bought it from a hard up student. The car was a bit inclined to make strange noises now and again but fortunately had not yet disgraced himself by breaking down.

'You know . . . I'm absolutely fed up with my job. If I don't get out of this rut before very long . . . I'll never get out of it. The only job I can do is typing and endless filing. If I have to file another batch of those cards like today I'll scream.' Melanie ended with a groan.

'No sooner said than done. We'll scan the papers tonight for you.'

Later that evening, settled comfortably on the sofa together, all papers were strewn across the floor in front of them, whilst they diligently scanned the adverts.

'Look, Melanie, the trouble with you

is that you aren't even looking in the right places. It isn't a clerical job you want to look for as you would only get bored with the same routine after a while. Now in my opinion there's a likely position here that I think you should try for.' The job was for a companion to a six year old girl for the duration of one year.

'Don't be ridiculous, I wouldn't know the first thing about being a companion. It sounds like something out of the Victorian era,' scoffed Melanie.

Anne would not be silenced. The address was up the Northumberland coast, a lovely part of the country, and not too far that they would lose contact with each other.

'At least write, for goodness sake, and get some further details from them.'

'Well alright, I will. The idea of looking after a little girl makes me feel a bit apprehensive, though, I think there's a glimmer of truth in what you are trying to say to me, Anne. In fact I'll send my application off, tonight.'

It was a beautiful, July morning and Melanie felt full of life and a sense of adventure as she drove up the motorway on her journey to her new job. She had duly sent her application that night and after only two days she had received her reply. The letter was from a Mrs. Kennedy, who appeared to be the housekeeper. She was acting on behalf of her employer, a Mr Masters, who was abroad for a few weeks. Therefore Mrs Kennedy was left with the business of engaging a companion for this man's daughter, who was named Chloe. The letter had gone on to state that she had telephoned Melanie's two referees who were the local vicar, a nice kindly family man who had known Melanie from birth, and one of her old school friends, who was now an infants teacher. Mrs Kennedy was apparently satisfied with these character references that had been given to her and informed

Melanie of salary details, which Melanie had thought quite generous. The letter also explained a little of the locality of Cliffe House, the Masters' residence in Beadnell. It became obvious that this housekeeper was warning her that it was a very quiet area and that to a city loving girl the place might seem too isolated and remote for her liking. Melanie was not disturbed at these revelations. The letter finished by letting Melanie know that the job was hers if she cared to ring a given telephone number within one day.

Anne could read Melanie's thoughts and knew that she was worrying about the upkeep of their flat.

'Don't worry about leaving this place. Judith who works in Admin. wants to sample life on her own for a while, away from home. I'm sure that she'll jump at the opportunity of coming here in your place.'

This seemed to decide Melanie to take the new job. After all, even if Judith did not stay then the generous salary would surely allow her a portion to send on to Anne if she couldn't afford the upkeep of the flat on her own.

Her thoughts resumed to the present; it couldn't be very long before the turning-off road for Beadnell village. An hour later she entered the village to look for Cliffe House. The local shopkeeper eventually gave her instructions for how to get there. Melanie pulled up outside a grey-stoned remote looking house bordered completely by large gardens, the smell and sound of the North Sea in the air around her. In fact the house was practically built on a prominent cliff overlooking the sea, observed Melanie as she waited at the door for someone to answer her knocks.

'Miss Crighton? Good morning, I'm Mrs Kennedy and I hope you had a good journey up. Leave your cases here, Mason will bring them in later.'

The hall was wide and oak panelled with a gracious staircase and several doors leading off into various reception rooms. They went through one of these doors into the lounge. It was a very large room with comfortable modern leather armchairs and sofas in cream with a matching deep pile carpet. The large sofas surrounded the imposing stone fireplace. After a tray of coffee had been brought in a few minutes later by the housekeeper Melanie studied Mrs Kennedy as she busied herself pouring the drink. She was a middle-aged woman, still attractive, with short, dark curly hair, dark skinned with light blue eyes.

'I'll be completely honest with you, dear, you were the only applicant for this job. That's why I wrote back to you for all you had no experience in this line of work. However, I always say, if you are young, and like children and don't mind being a bit out of the way of things, well, I don't see any difficulties.' Mrs Kennedy gave a warm, encouraging smile to Melanie. 'Mr Masters is your employer although he left things in my hands about getting someone for

Chloe, he had to return to the States where we have all been living for the past five years. Anyway, he's due back anytime in the next few days. Chloe had pneumonia a few months ago, it was when we first arrived here, in fact, so you'll find her a little weak and you'll have to be careful that she doesn't do anything strenuous for the present. Her father wants her to convalesce for a year then she'll be going away to school.'

After they had finished their coffee, she was shown upstairs to her room. Melanie was enchanted with her bedroom; it appeared to be at the back of the house but there was a beautiful view from the window of the Cheviots and the fine gardens below. The furniture was modern with white fitted units and the colours of the carpet and curtains were in restful dusky pinks and browns. There was a comfortable window seat and Melanie thought she would be able to relax easily here. She was left to unpack and lost in her thoughts she didn't notice anyone enter the open door. Swinging round suddenly, after catching sight of a reflection in the mirror unit, of a small dark-haired little girl. 'Hello . . . you must be Chloe. I'm very pleased to meet you, I'm called Melanie and I think it's very nice of you to come and greet me.'

Chloe just stood there, hovering in the doorway. She was a lovely child, brown hair, dark sun-tanned skin, brown eyes. She obviously had spent a lot of time outdoors recently and didn't look frail at all. A nut-brown little elf, thought Melanie. Chloe was gazing in an unfriendly way at her.

'Auntie Rose says you're gonna look after me,' said a small accusing voice.

Auntie Rose must be the housekeeper, Mrs Kennedy, thought Melanie. 'I've brought you a present, Chloe, I got it in Durham which is where I live. Have you ever been there?' As she spoke to the child she withdrew from her open case a small rag doll, and handed the gift over to the child. Chloe seemed to be delighted with her surprise present and Melanie was rewarded with a cheeky smile.

'What about a helping hand with my unpacking, hmm?'

'Sure,' came the instant reply.

They chatted on happily for the next hour as Melanie sorted her clothes away and she discovered that the child had no friends of the same age; in fact, there was only Daddy, Mason, the gardener and Auntie Rose, the house-keeper.

Later, after Chloe had been put to bed by Rose, they watched television in the lounge. The older woman outlined the arrangements to her that she, not Melanie, would see to Chloe in the morning and that she would also put Chloe to bed every evening. Therefore Melanie would look after the child from after breakfast until suppertime. They retired early, Rose through habit and Melanie because she was travel weary. She wondered how Chloe's father could leave such an important decision as choosing his child's companion in the hands of the housekeeper. These thoughts kept her occupied as she prepared for bed: where was the mother? No mention by any of the household of a Mrs Masters. She shrugged away her nagging unease; it was going to be an interesting job and their private affairs were no concern of hers anyway.

The next few days, the weather being glorious, Chloe and Melanie explored the village. Its harbour was small and further along was a large, sandy bay, sheltered, and on a sunny day a wonderful place to lie and sunbathe or paddle in the sea. Numerous dunes surrounded the beach and they spent endless, amusing hours pottering about the dunes. Chloe acquired an even deeper tan and Melanie caught the sun too. She felt a great affection for the child, perhaps engendered by the fact of Chloe's loneliness and sensitivity. One day they were returning after another day on the beach to the house when Rose greeted them in the drive as she was on her way down to the village.

'Mr Masters has just sent a cable. He'll be returning late tonight sometime.' She turned to Chlo.e 'You'll see your daddy in the morning, love.'

The two women waited up that evening until near midnight and still he had not returned. Sadly, the housekeeper decided to retire for the night.

'He won't be very pleased if he finds us waiting for him in the early hours, so we may as well get our sleep too.'

In the early hours of the morning, Melanie was awoken by the sounds of a car being put in the garages at the side of the house. Footsteps sounded across the patio and she heard the back door being opened. Sleepily she turned over and pulling the covers over her head realized Chloe's father had returned home. The next morning, she dressed with great care, eager to make a good impression with her new employer. Instead of denim shorts, sun top and bikini underneath, which had been her daily attire recently, pale green canvas trousers and a cream blouse were donned. She felt cool and composed but as she slowly descended the stairs to the kitchen, where they all gathered for breakfast, nervous excitement fluttered in the region of her stomach.

Only Chloe and Rose were in the kitchen: Melanie, after greeting them, took her place at the table. The housekeeper eyed her outfit, noticing her change of apparel and, raising her eyebrows, stared at Melanie.

'Mr Masters would like to see you after your breakfast, Melanie. He'll be in his study,' said Rose.

Chloe had already invaded the study but her Daddy had told her to get her meal and not to disturb him until later, the child informed Melanie. She felt unaccountably nervous as she hovered outside the study door a few minutes later. What's the matter with me? Heavens, he was only a man. She knocked quickly and at the sound of a man's deep voice bidding her enter, she opened the door to reveal a tall man with his back towards her, looking out of the window, her only view. As she slowly walked into the centre of the room she vaguely felt that there was something familiar about the man. He turned to greet her, and with a gasp of dismay, Melanie realized that he was the man with the scar. The man who had rescued her from that odious bore, the night she had gone to York, a few weeks previously. They both faced each other and she knew that Jake Masters had also recognized her and by the expression on his face, it bode no good for Melanie Crighton.

2

'Oh no,' she breathed. For several seconds her employer simply stared at Melanie, with a look of surprise and, she thought uneasily, contempt. She felt unable to gather her confused thoughts to cope with the interview that was about to commence. Yet for all her powers of thought and speech were frozen and silent, her bemused brain could still admire the sheer maleness of this man. She felt a bundle of nerves, like a puppet, standing before him waiting for Jake Masters to make the first move, or utter the first words, and then she would be prompted into an action of some sort.

'Good morning, Miss Crighton, I can see that we have both instantly recognized each other.'

His speech was short and the words cut through her like a whiplash, for she visibly winced. Damn the man.

He indicated a chair in front of his desk and as she seated herself, he strolled round to the other side and sat facing her. His attire did not help to relax the atmosphere, a very different garb from the last time she had seen him. From the casual to the strictly conventional, dressed in a black suit, perfectly tailored, blue shirt and matching tie, although the style of his clothes was very much up to the minute in the fashion world. His hair looked longer, growing well down the back of his neck, thickly brushing his collar, but on the whole he presented a very attractive appearance, and his satanic looking scar adding just the right dash of mystery to his person. Jake Masters looked down at her with such a superior air that it was coaxing Melanie's temper to rise slowly but surely.

'I'm afraid that I'd like to be completely frank with you Miss Crighton, and state that had I been able to conduct the interviews for this position you hold, you would not indeed be honouring my house with your presence.'

'If you're referring to that night in York I would like to put the facts right about it, really . . . the . . . '

'I don't wish to hear the personal details of your love life,' Jake cut in as Melanie hesitated in framing her explanation.

'Very well, Mr Masters, then speak to Mrs Kennedy, speak to Chloe. I'm sure that you'll find a great change for the better with regards to Chloe. Why . . . you only have to look at her to see the difference since I arrived here.'

Jake opened his mouth to interrupt her again but Melanie was not to be put off. 'Chloe has changed from the shy little introvert into a normal perky little girl.'

'There's no need to go on. I've already had your virtues extolled from my daughter earlier this morning. I'm sorry . . . but I feel that you are not the person suited for the job. Naturally you shall receive a month's wages in advance for your trouble.

To save the need for any scenes from Chloe, I would appreciate it very much if you left here as soon as possible.'

How dare he, had the man no feelings? She certainly wouldn't work for the insufferable pig that he was.

'These aren't Victorian times . . . it's 1975 and your attitude is ridiculous. I won't even waste any more time or breath. Keep your wages for the next poor unsuspecting girl you employ. She'll certainly have my sympathy.'

Melanie stormed out of the study and made straight for her room before the tears that were welling up in her eyes could spill over. She was trembling with rage and, at the same time, bitterly disappointed at the outcome of her interview. Blindly, she started to pack her cases, throwing her clothes in any jumbled way. The tears, her reaction to the heated exchange in the study, now falling quickly down her cheeks, she could hardly see what she was packing.

She was sitting quietly on the bed as she heard a light tap on the door and

Rose quickly entered with an envelope in her hand. She took one look at Melanie's distressed face and her eyes clouded with sympathy and puzzlement. She sat on the other side of Melanie's case.

'I don't understand. Jake is in an icy temper. In fact I daren't say a word; it's a long time since I saw him in that state. What went wrong?' She looked down at the envelope in her hand. 'He's asked me to give you this, said it was your wages and that you're leaving.' She faltered at the last words and looked across at Melanie, waiting for the explanation. Melanie, however, had had enough of the Master's menage and quietly told the housekeeper to return the cheque to Mr Masters; and with this simple request, quickly gathered her case and bag and made for the door.

★   ★   ★

As she reversed her car out of the big garage, resisting the childish impulse to bump into the sleek dark red Jensen that obviously belonged to that 'insufferable pig', as she labelled him, her eyes caught sight of Chloe. She was talking to Mason, the gardener, outside one of his greenhouses, although she couldn't read the expression on the child's face from that distance, by the manner in which she stood, tensed and still, she knew Chloe had guessed that there was something wrong. Melanie couldn't bear the thought of saying goodbye to Chloe; she was glad that the child had not seen her upset in her bedroom. It could leave a bad impression on the child and upset relations between father and daughter. The very thought of the child started her tears afresh, and with a great effort of trying to pull herself together she concentrated on driving the car along the drive, not looking in her rear mirror once until she had driven on to the main road.

The village looked the same as she passed through, people walking along the street with no evidence of disaster on their faces. The salty tang of the sea still pervaded the air; the gulls screamed above on their restless errands. Nothing had changed, only the girl in the car felt that her world had crashed around her. How she longed to see Anne again. Her flatmate would make light work of this episode and put life back in its right perspective for Melanie.

The country lanes had been left behind after half an hour and she turned on to the main road for Newcastle. After a few minutes' driving, she glanced in her rear mirror and saw the dark red car loom up behind her. Melanie's heart missed several beats; what on earth was he doing? He must want to see her. The thought of speaking to Jake Masters in such short time positively unnerved her. She could see his stern face behind the wheel and then he flashed his lights, several times, at her. She could hardly concentrate on her driving, her pulse hammering erractically, and then quickly he had overtaken her car and was indicating that they pull in to the side of the road.

She suppressed the giggle that started to bubble up in her throat as she recognized it not for humour, more hysteria, due to the shock of finding him pursuing her. He reached her car as she was in the act of getting out of the driving seat, and as their eyes met, his were the first to look away. He looked guiltily at her for a moment and then, as if shaking this feeling from him, he squared his broad shoulders and clearly asked her to return to Beadnell with him.

At first there was a stunned silence, her mind still registering the fact that her new job was still in existence. The traffic was continually passing them, although she was hardly conscious of their noise. She continued to stare at him, looking for a clue as to why the change of heart. His face remained impassive, his grey eyes as cool as a winter's day, but his scar seemed whiter against the bronze skin of his face.

'Well?' Jake stirred the still, electric atmosphere with his terse monosyllable. Melanie almost jumped and at the same time answered, 'Yes.'

'I'm afraid Chloe went into a right old tantrum as apparently she saw you leave the house. She came rushing to see me to find out the reason for your departure. I've never seen her in such a hysterical state before. You seem to have made a deeper impression on her than I gave you credit for. She seems to rely on you . . . only my answer that I would come and see you would calm her down. As you know, she's still not fit and I don't like to see her as distressed as this.'

As they drew their cars into the driveway of Cliffe House, Chloe had spotted them from the lounge window. The child ran out to meet them, clutched in her arms the rag doll that Melanie had given her on their meeting. The unmistakable signs were of the recent tears on her face, now flushed with joy that Melanie had returned with her father. Melanie felt awkward with him as he carried her case up the stairs back to her room. As they entered her room Chloe was bouncing happily on the bed.

'Daddy, let's go to the beach after lunch. The three of us, this afternoon.'

'I'm sorry pet, but I must go through my papers in the study this afternoon.' He turned to Melanie standing awkwardly in the centre of the room. 'In fact, Miss Crighton, I shall be very busy during the next few days and would be most grateful if you keep Chloe out of my study.'

How unfair of him, she thought to herself, he didn't deserve the love and adoration his daughter felt for him. He selfishly didn't want to indulge her with his valuable time but his eyes bore into hers, almost as a challenge to query his demand for solitude. Go carefully, my girl, let's get established back here first, then we'll see what's what.

'Very well, Mr Masters. I'll try to keep Chloe out of your hair.' She couldn't resist the last few words but he merely raised his eyebrows in reply and, turning, left the room.

★ ★ ★

For three weeks the weather continued its glorious sunshine, which Melanie and her small charge made the most of by continual sessions on the beach or short rambles along the nearby country lanes. Sometimes Melanie took Chloe off in Hercules, her ever faithful 'banger', for short rides up and down the coast. She never trusted the car to drive too far afield in case of breakdowns. Her opinion of these parts of the North East were that it was a beautiful region; the border counties had an atmosphere of brooding violence and one could sense the past battles that had been furiously fought there between the English and Scots. It was a delight to stroll along the narrow lanes bordering the wild countryside, with the overpowering scent of honey-suckle that clung to the hedges invading their senses. The surrounding farmlands were ready to yield their summer harvest and the men were all busy in the fields working. Many would raise their hands in salute at the pair as they wandered around the lanes and cut across the fields, looking for the inevitable mice that darted amongst the corn stubble after the harvester had devastated their nests.

Of Jake Masters, Melanie saw very little. to her surprise the housekeeper had told her that Jake was a song composer. He was something of a celebrity in the States and had written several hit musicals there. The music room, specially soundproofed, adjoined his study; Melanie had never been there but knew Jake spent many hours daily within its walls. She liked his music, especially the romantic ballads, but had never realized that he was this particular composer. Rose had given her more personal information about Jake. His wife was very much alive and famous in her own right in the ballet world. Jake and his wife, Marion, had separated shortly after Chloe had been born. They lived their own lives, she in London, but they were not divorced. To the housekeeper's knowledge, Marion had never visited her daughter, or Jake, since the separation.

Melanie had ample opportunity to talk to Rose as every evening they would sit in the lounge watching the television when Chloe had been put to bed. Jake rarely joined them. The Jensen was often seen by them going out of the drive after dinner with Jake behind the wheel. Where he went Melanie never knew. The rare times that he decided to join them in the lounge, she had never felt at ease. Many times she would interrupt an enigmatic glance from him. Usually she would retire early to bed on these occasions.

Her thoughts were troubled on her employer's attitude towards his daughter. They spent a little time together each morning, Jake and Chloe, whilst Melanie breakfasted and had her morning chat with Rose. After that Jake was either working or out. Chloe didn't seem to mind his absence, obviously she was used to this, but it irked Melanie somewhat. It really was no concern of hers and should she voice her thoughts to him, she would surely be told this is in no uncertain manner. That was until she heard that Chloe's birthday would be celebrated in a couple of weeks.

Rose Kennedy started off the chain of events that tipped Melanie's safe little world crazily on its axis. They were enjoying their evening chat, Chloe was in bed and Jake had, as usual, gone out for the evening. The weather had changed and it was a wet and windy night. Darkness had fallen early due to the heavy, grey clouds that had hung persistently through the day. The fire had been lit in the lounge and the pair of them were relaxing comfortably on the sofas enjoying a cigarette; they were both mesmerized by the dancing flames in the fireplace. A contented silence hung over them, apart from the sounds of the licking flames hungrily consuming the logs, the rain on the window lashing the glass at frequent intervals with the squally gusts of wind.

'Melanie, I don't know whether Chloe has said anything to you but she will be seven years old in two week's time. I thought I would have a day off to shop in Newcastle on Friday. I'll get her the presents . . . I usually get Jake's present for him. He's so busy, you know. Mind you he decides whatever it is he wants for her. If there's anything I can get for you . . . just let me know.'

Melanie thanked her for the offer, expressing surprise about the coming birthday and commented that she would have to think of a suitable gift for the child. Rose continued to gaze into the fire as she went on, 'He's asked me to get her a watch this time. She'll be 'over the moon' when she gets it.' Rose smiled into the fire, imagining the child's face on opening the present. She sighed, 'Unfortunately her father may not be here to see it as he mentioned to me that he has been invited away for that weekend; a house party somewhere near Cambridge, I think.'

Big deal. Fancy not spending the day with his own daughter. Well it only proved to her just how little he could be bothered with his child. Melanie's blood pressure rose at the thoughts of his selfishness, it rose even further as her mind ticked over on resolving what course of action she was determined to take on Chloe's behalf. Considering the task before her she lost the trend of what Rose was asking her.

'I beg your pardon, what was that you said?'

Rose smiled at Melanie. 'I thought you had gone off in a trance. Have you anything in mind for Chloe's present?'

'Oh, I think a set of watercolour paints and some drawing materials would be a nice idea, don't you think? . . . They would have come in very handy for her on a rotten day such as it's been today.'

The older woman agreed with her decision. 'I'll be happy to get them for you, dear. Jake is driving me to the station . . . I don't know whether he will be in for dinner but I shall prepare a cold meat salad, just in case.'

At Melanie's puzzled glance she explained that she would be staying at friends in Newcastle overnight and would return before lunchtime Saturday. It wasn't often that she got the chance to have such a nice break and now that Melanie was in the house she could leave Chloe knowing she was 'in safe hands'. Melanie assured her that she would look after things during her absence. Privately she hoped Jake Masters would not be around all day or that would make her nervous, as was the usual effect of his presence.

* * *

Friday arrived, the weather still showery although this morning the brave sun was peeking out from the scattered clouds. Outside ventures off today, thought Melanie glumly. She bade the housekeeper goodbye after breakfast, and told her to enjoy herself. Chloe went with her father as he drove Rose to the station. She waved them all off at the front porch; they would not return until lunchtime, around one o'clock. Earlier Jake had entered the kitchen to ask Melanie if she would like to accompany them for a ride into Seahouses, a small coastal resort not far up the coast. She had panicked at the idea of being with him; she became tongue-tied normally with him so the thoughts of a couple of hours of his undiluted company would be unendurable to her. In any case, it would be a good thing for father and daughter to enjoy their own private outing. She declined his invitation, making the excuse to catch up on her correspondence to friends and relations back home.

'Incidentally,' Jake cleared his throat to go on, 'I've been too busy to mention it earlier, but anytime you yourself want a weekend home . . . just let me know. You haven't had any time off at all since you . . . er, came here.' His eyes were more blue than grey today, warmer somehow. He didn't look directly at her face, he focussed his attention to a point somewhere above her head. The thought caused her to smile and then flush as his gaze fell to her own eyes.

'We'll be back for one and have our lunch together, the three of us. If that's alright with you?' At her nod he continued, 'Rustle up something simple and quick as I'll be working later and want to get on as soon as possible.' And then Jake smiled at her, a warm smile that changed his countenance com- pletely. He looked younger, more approachable, and it affected Melanie to give him a warm smile in return. She thought how attractive he was today, dressed in cream cotton jeans and shirt, open at the neck to reveal a small part of his tanned chest, suspiciously dark with hairs which enhanced his masculine appearance.

She realized he was waiting for some sort of reply from her as he got out his cigarettes and after lighting one slowly looked at her, exhaling the smoke. 'Er . . . yes . . . surely, Mr Masters . . . about one o'clock then?' she queried. She roused herself into some sort of action of trying to clear the crockery from the kitchen table without dropping anything under his close scrutiny.

'Fine,' and after a pause, 'and there's no need for formalities, the name's Jake, okay?' He left the kitchen without waiting for her reply.

After the Jensen had disappeared out of view, Melanie turned to go back into the house. A feeling of restlessness came over her. She wandered into the kitchen to finish her task. After leaving the room spotless she ventured into the garden. Mason was nowhere to be seen, probably down the local or around the harbour talking to his old cronies she mused. Even the garden wasn't a pleasant place to be wandering about today; the lawn was soggy underfoot after the previous day's rain. Everything had a dashed look about it, the roses slightly dishevelled, the trees with a hanging, sodden appearance. The smell of damp earth pervaded everywhere. She retreated to the comfort of the lounge and attempted the 'Times' crossword. An hour later she gave it up in disgust, hardly any clues solved.

Could she be bored? Surely not because the house was empty. Or perhaps it was because Jake usually filled it with his vibrant personality, that he coloured her environment. Surely not, she murmered, talking to herself. She decided to check the bedrooms in case Rose had not made the beds that morning. So she made her way to the housekeeper's room which she found to be in immaculate order. On she went to

Chloe's room and after clearing away the scattered toys — and some hesitation — she glanced into Jake's bedroom. She had never been inside his room before and felt her palms moisten nervously as if she were about to do something wrong. Shaking off this queer feeling of guilt she walked right into the room.

It was an absolute shambles, causing her to smile at his typically male untidy habits. Looking around her, it was a large room, situated at the front of the house, overlooking the sea. In servant's jargon it would have been termed the 'master bedroom'. It was very attractive with its dark rosewood wall fitments covering one wall entirely, the apricot walls, deep pile cream carpet and brown curtains and bedspread matching perfectly. She stooped to pick up Jake's discarded clothes that looked as if he had flung them on the floor and was in the act of retrieving a silk shirt she had overlooked when the aroma of cigarette smoke teased her nostrils.

Swinging round she met Jake's eyes as he lounged against the door jamb, a lighted cigarette in his hand and a lazy smile on his face.

Melanie visibly started and tried to swallow down her dry throat as he advanced towards her. 'I thought I'd tidy up the bedrooms as Mrs Kennedy wouldn't have had time this morning,' she stammered apologetically. She felt terrible, as if she had invaded his privacy; ridiculous really, somebody had to make the beds, what was the matter with her? She scolded herself for acting silly.

'That's alright Melanie, thanks.' He strolled over to the window and looked out. As the shock of his sudden appearance subsided, she could feel her face starting to burn with embarrassment. She turned away and mumbled on about putting the discarded clothes in the linen basket for washing and walked towards the door. The deep carpet hushed any footfalls and so it was with a start she felt his hand on her bare arm.

'Don't look so guilty, Melanie. Thanks for putting my room straight . . . I know I'm an untidy devil,' he said with a slight chuckle, his steady gaze on her face.

'I'm starving Melanie. What's for lunch?' demanded Chloe as she stampeded into the room like a baby elephant, thought Melanie. 'We saw Auntie Rose off and then went for a lovely walk along the beach . . . didn't we Daddy?' The delicate atmosphere was broken and Melanie hastened out of the room, down the stairs with Chloe tramping down behind her asking if she could help make the lunch with her.

Jake, to Melanie's relief, after thanking her for a delightful meal, took himself off to his study. She basked in the warm feeling of satisfaction from his compliments about her cooking; she had taken great care with the grilled steaks. Normally they turned out like morsels of charred meat at home whenever she and Anne had cooked them.

'I won't be going out tonight . . . but don't bother with dinner for me. I'll raid the larder when I'm hungry, okay?' as he walked towards the door.

'Fine,' was her reply. Oh no, were her thoughts. If he stays in the lounge tonight I daren't plead another head-ache. Never mind how pleasant he'd been towards her today. Nothing to worry about, in fact, maybe it would be a good time to tackle him about the picnic idea. She felt quite confident about approaching him on the subject as Chloe helped her clear away the plates. She wasn't going to say anything to Chloe until the matter had been settled.

★ ★ ★

Putting the child to bed was a novelty Melanie thoroughly enjoyed. The noise the pair of them made that echoed around Chloe's bathroom was of unlimited laughter. It took quite some time before Chloe's eyes became heavy with sleep, and only after Melanie had exhausted her repetoire of old nursery tales did she succumb to the arms of Morpheus. Melanie felt her heart melt with affection as she looked down on the sleeping child; Chloe's thick brown hair spread about her elfin face, her long eyelashes hiding her eyes, eyes that could widen as big as saucers when she was excited about anything. She stooped over the child and kissed her lightly on the brow, whispering a goodnight to her.

'Night Mel'nie,' came the blurred reply. Quietly Melanie left the room.

There was no sign of Jake as yet, and she guessed he wouldn't be making an appearance for a while yet. Deciding to have her meal in solitary state in the kitchen, she retired to her own room to bathe and change. The dress she was wearing was soaked due to the half hour session in the bathroom with Chloe. Her hair also was damp and, collecting some clean clothes, she stole along to the bathroom. Melanie enjoyed the next hour, relaxing in a hot bath, the water liberally sprinkled with bath salts of which there was always a plentiful supply on the shelf above the bath. Towelling herself dry, she reflected on the best way to broach the subject of Chloe's birthday to her father. Her heartbeats started to race in nervous anticipation, although she calmed herself yet again with the thought of his changed manner of today. A newer, gentler Jake, who didn't look on her any longer with icy disdain.

She dressed in light blue canvas jeans and a soft white wool sweater. No make up, she decided, her face felt wonderfully clean and tingling after her unhurried toilet. Her hair she left hanging down her back as it was still damp from her shampoo, and with a final brush of her hair she left her room and descended the stairs to the kitchen.

Melanie hadn't realized how hungry she was until she saw the appetizing dish of chicken and salad in the fridge. She was in the act of cutting several thick slices of fresh baked crusty bread when Jake's head appeared around the kitchen door.

'My . . . aren't we slumming tonight? It's well seen the housekeeper's away.'

'We agreed a scratch meal when we felt like it,' she retorted defensively.

'Okay, okay . . . don't get so shirty, I was only kidding. I've interrupted my work as I'm starving. How about making me some of that,' as he pointed to her salad, 'and we'll eat in here.'

She looked at him, saying nothing, then set about preparing a place for him at the table. She was unaware of the attractive picture she looked. Her fine black hair, almost dry now, framing her small honey tanned face. He watched her as she moved from the fridge to the table with the bowl of salad and chicken. Had she but looked up at him she would have interpreted his glance of appreciation of her graceful form, bending to her tasks.

Jake felt his nerves relaxing with the quiet movements of the girl as she prepared the meal. God, how peaceful to be in feminine company that wasn't the cloying type or the predatory kind of female. Since Marion had ensnared him in marriage, which had been a disaster from the word 'go', his feelings towards women were exceedingly cynical. Not that he avoided them for they had their uses, but to his jaded eyes they were, all of them, bitches. His mind flashed to various instances when he himself had acted callously towards his female acquaintances. He had doled out whatever they deserved, but this girl, she looked only a child with her scrubbed face, shining clean hair flowing down her back. Melanie didn't flaunt her charms boldly as he would have expected from her.

'Sit down and have your meal, Jake.' Her soft voice broke his reverie and brought himself to awareness of his surroundings. They ate their meal in silence. After they had cleared their plates with hungry enjoyment, they lazed back in their armchairs drinking the coffee, Jake with his feet raised on a stool. He lit a cigarette and watched Melanie exhaling smoke from her cigarette.

'That was a lovely meal. I certainly needed it. Er . . . I hope you don't mind my slovenly habits,' he added as he indicated his feet relaxing on the stool.

Melanie smiled warmly at him. 'Not at all, it's your home. Would you like some more coffee?' As she rose to get another cup she thought he had a strained and tired look about him today. He's probably working too hard and could do with a break, she thought sympathetically. 'Tell me about your music, Jake. What are you working on at the moment?'

'Ah now kitten, I never discuss work . . . especially after a hard day of it. Talk to me instead about yourself. I'm interested,' he drawled.

At first she was stilted in her speech and then as she relaxed in his company she became more expansive. She recounted to him her memories of early childhood with her parents. Then the time of living with her aunt and her large family, and her subsequent branching out, living on her own, finishing with a description of her flatmate Anne, and the series of escapades which they had usually got themselves into, in the past.

He was fascinated watching her, Melanie's face was animated, her eyes sparkling with remembered humorous episodes. She was so young and fresh, and for once, acting naturally with him. It was such a change for he had noticed the tense way she would react when he was in the same room as her.

'You're not listening to me, are you?' Her voice, once again, broke in on his thoughts.

'Of course I am, kitten. I can tell you everything you've just said to me.'

'Don't call me that, I don't like it,' she lied, typically female.

Jake smiled, his eyes looking straight into her own. 'But I can't help it, sometimes you look a small defenceless, quiet thing, then all of a sudden your claws are lashing out when I least expect it. Like, er . . . now. Kitten,' he finished softly.

Melanie was confused at this exchange of words between them. She recognized the basic charm he could display, as he was doing now, making her feelings disturbed to such an extent that, to break this delicate atmosphere, she stood up to clear away the plates. Jake, too, stood up and after some hesitation, he offered his services as assistant dish washer. Melanie turned an amazed face at him, saying she would manage better on her own.

'Well, I'll tidy up those papers I've been working on today,' and, turned, leaving her to her chores.

Making sure the kitchen was left clean and spotless for the housekeeper's return, she looked at the clock and surprisingly saw it was only nine thirty. A bit early to retire for the night, and after a slight hesitation, she made her way to the lounge to watch television.

She found Jake sprawled along one of the sofas, a drink in his hand, watching television. As soon as she entered the lounge he started to get to his feet and lazily strolled over to the tray of drinks, asking her what she would like. After Melanie had accepted a martini, they sat down opposite each other on the sofas. The play on the set was one of those monotonous kitchen sink dramas, the type Melanie detested. She couldn't interest herself in it and sat taking nervous sips of her drink.

Now's the time to mention the picnic she thought, and as she tried to mentally rehearse the most suitable words to broach the matter, she could feel her throat drying up and her heart thudding. She tried to calm herself down and, turning to face him, realized that Jake, too, hadn't been watching television, he was staring at herself.

'Jake . . . as you know, it's Chloe's birthday soon. I think she would be so pleased if you took her on a picnic that day. It would be a real treat for her. She rarely sees you and to her, there's nobody in the world like her daddy. Couldn't you do this for her?' Melanie had rushed her sharp little sentences before her breath gave out with nerves. Jake's eyes hardened in expression, turning from the warm blue colour back to their usual cool grey. She wasn't going to give up now so before he could say anything she blindly rushed on, 'Chloe only sees you for a short while after breakfast . . . really it's not enough.'

'Just what are you implying? I don't need you to tell me how to bring up my daughter.' His tone was harsh and he gulped his drink off only to go over to the drinks tray and pour another stiff measure of whisky.

'When I first came here, I got the impression that Chloe was a very lonely person. She was very shy with me at first. I expected that, but her loneliness was unnatural. Please take her on this outing, Jake, I'm sure it will mean so much to her,' she pleaded at him.

'Look, mind your own damn business. Don't try to tell me about my daughter or what I should or should not do. I pay you generously for looking after her and don't you forget that this job got you out of your little rut as you told me earlier tonight. And if you're staying on here there's one little rule you'll have to observe. I can't stand females telling me how to run my life.' He snarled the last few words at her almost and Melanie's face whitened with the shock of his onslaught. Heavens, she thought, this conversation had snowballed completely out of proportion. His reference to her own personal situation of taking this job had really hurt her and she also experienced a few stabs of guilt. There was an element of truth in his accusation. The tears, she knew, were not far from welling up in her eyes and as he moodily finished off his drink, only to replenish his glass again, she hastily placed her drink on the table behind her and with a muttered 'goodnight' to

Jake left the room.

She flung herself on the bed facing the ceiling, swallowing quickly; her throat was aching with the force of the tears that slid pathetically down her cheeks. She realized that she was indulging more in self pity than the fact that Chloe would not have the outing, but he had been so nice to her today and to have him berate her so harshly filled her with a feeling of despondency and made the tears fall faster than ever. For weeks they had lived in relative harmony, and now what would be the outcome of this, thought Melanie miserably.

So absorbed was she in her turbulent thoughts, the tap on the door went unheard. Suddenly she was aware of Jake slowly walking towards her bed. His face wore a guilty expression and she hastily turned onto her stomach, hiding her face from him. Her whole skin felt hot at the mess she must look in this distressed state.

'Go away . . . please,' she whispered,

not trusting her voice any louder in case it disgraced her further by breaking with her disturbed emotions. She felt the bed give way as he slowly lowered himself onto it. Then, gently, he pulled her round to face him, holding her shoulders in his hands, his touch searing. He said, almost in a whisper, 'I'm sorry, truly, Melanie. I think maybe you were telling me too many home truths and I guess that's why I lost my head, honey. We'll go on that picnic, the three of us, that's a promise.' Then, after a long pause, 'I don't like to see you hurt, kitten . . . come on . . . cheer up, hmm?' His cool, lean fingers traced a tear softly, and the gentle touch on her face was making her stomach leap alarmingly.

To Jake, the sight of her wan face, glistening with tears, her eyes large and reproachful, disturbed his peace of mind, a thought he acknowledged with some surprise. Her dark hair was spread out in tumbled profusion on the bed and he could not resist the compelling urge to touch it. Suddenly, the atmosphere changed. Even the air became still and quiet in the room. She noticed Jake's breathing alter, become slower and louder, as she tried to stop her heart beating at such an alarming rate. She couldn't resist looking up into his eyes, that seemed nearer all of a sudden. His lazy, sensuous gaze travelled down her face to stop at her mouth, lingering there; her own lips parted automatically, as if he had physically touched them with his own. They were very aware of the close proximity of their bodies, Melanie could feel the heat of his skin and was disturbed by the clean, spicy, male tang of him. Jake leaned over her and gently caressed the side of her face with his fingers; trailing around her lips, she could smell a faint trace of whisky on his breath and she wondered how much he had had to drink tonight.

Her eyes moved to his scar which she could see was throbbing on the side of his face. Never had she seen it in close detail, starting from his strong brow, just missing his right eyebrow and tapering off into his thick hair. It was a fascinating mark, that made her fingers tremble at the thought of tracing its outline. A muscle in the side of his cheek moved as his jaw tightened. Jake gave an audible groan of regret or perhaps self-disgust and with a sudden movement that took her by surprise, he stood up. For a few seconds he just stared down at her and then turned and walked purposefully to the door.

'We'll talk about it tomorrow,' he said, his voice deep and husky, and then, 'Goodnight, kitten.'

At first Melanie wondered what he meant and then realized he was referring to the outing. She couldn't find her voice to answer him at all as he quietly closed the door behind him. Melanie turned her hot face into the pillows, unable to analyse her emotions. Never had she felt so disturbed at a male presence in such close proximity to her own. Animal magnetism, sheer sexual attraction; let's face it, Jake certainly has got what it takes, she debated. And then she remembered the silent interchange that had taken place' it was an ecstasy to feel the raw emotion and she knew without a doubt that Jake had also been affected. Their relationship would never be the same again, and what the outcome would be she hardly dared to guess at, but he had a wife . . . albeit they weren't living together, but she existed, they weren't divorced.

Slowly Melanie sat up on the bed, staring unseeingly into space. She had never let her feelings about any man rule over her common sense before and she was determined that she would not get involved with this man. She remembered again, wistfully, the feel of his strong hands, the clean scent of him as he leaned over her. She would never forget the look in those slumberous eyes that had almost drowned her own in their enigmatic depths, as blue and as deep as the ocean. She must chase these memories away as she got up to undress for bed. Sliding between the sheets later, she knew that it would be a very difficult thing for her to do, oh so difficult.

3

It was a hot day and the sunshine was a caressing warmth on Melanie's bikini-clad body as she lay drowsily on the beach. The nearby murmur of children's voices reassured her that Chloe was in safe hands. There was a picnic party on the beach, a family from the city. Their infectious gaiety and engaging impish faces of the children had drawn Chloe, welcomingly, into their exclusive circle, to build the 'biggest sandcastle ever made'. This they had tackled with serious industry and the mother of the family, a Mrs Allen, had come over to where Melanie lay to reassure her that the 'little girl' would be well supervised. 'Dinna worry, hinny, the little girl is safe with my lot,' and grinning broadly at Melanie she returned to the heap of children to settle down comfortably back to her knitting.

Melanie felt tired and hoped that she would snooze, basking in the sun's warmth. Idly she sifted the fine sand through her fingers as she closed her eyes and settled down on the beachtowel. No wonder she was tired, the number of successive sleepless nights she had tossed and turned in her bed until the faint lightening of dawn threaded its way through the sky. Only then did she seemingly drift off into an uneasy sleep, that left her heavy-eyed most mornings. Why, oh why, couldn't she get Jake out of her mind? It was almost a week now since Rose had gone off to Newcastle for that day. Melanie had hardly seen anything of Jake since the morning he had brought Rose back from the station. Even at meal times he rarely put in an appearance; at which times he wasn't there at the table, Melanie would feel deflated for reasons that she hardly dared ask herself. When Jake did turn up, Melanie felt tongue-tied and awkward in his company. Frequently she interrupted Rose in the act of preparing trays of food for him to be eaten in his study. Really it was these absences that worried her, thinking, perhaps, that due to her behaviour that night they quarrelled, she had disgusted him. She admitted to herself that she found him attractive, no, fascinating, but she had no confidence in her own appeal. Again and again she argued mentally that it was his realization after that fateful night, when, in her room, Jake had discovered she was attracted to him, and he was subsequently making himself scarce because of this. There again, she would superimpose these thoughts with the fact that such a celebrity as Jake would merely find her infatuation, for that would be his name for it, amusing from such a nonentity as Melanie Crighton, and then probably become bored with the whole idea. Hence his sudden immersion in his work again.

'Hello there.'

Melanie abruptly sat up as Jake's eyes roved appreciatively over her body.

'Oh . . . you gave me a fright. I was sound asleep,' she lied as she looked up at him, having to screw her eyes against the sun. She felt at a disadvantage at his towering height, unable to read the expression on his face as he had his back to the sun.

'Er . . . your daughter's over there,' she added as she pointed to the enormous sandcastle in progress.

'I know. I've just been speaking to them all.'

'Oh.' She was a little bewildered by his arrival on the beach. A thing he had never done before and she wondered why he was here now. As Jake sat down beside her and stretched his full length out to the sun's rays, she took the opportunity to gaze at him appreciatively. Navy denim shorts and a short sleeved blue shirt, open at the front down to his waist which revealed a broad, muscled chest, liberally covered in black hair. his eyes were closed and her gaze travelled back to his face to settle on his scar. After a few moments Jake's eyes suddenly flew open and caught her staring.

'It bothers you doesn't it?' he said as he pointed to the scar. Melanie's face flamed and tingles of awareness of his close proximity and low, intimate voice played havoc up and down her spine.

'Of course not. It's just intriguing, that's all,' was her quick retort.

Jake slowly got to his feet, not taking his eyes from her own for one instant, and Melanie seemed mesmerized by his locking gaze. Lazily, he peeled off his shirt and shorts to reveal blue swimming gear underneath and as he reached for her hand to draw Melanie to her feet he murmured, 'Well, don't be . . . it's a boyhood scar and I deserved it for scaling dangerous cliffs which could have caused my death. Come and swim with me.'

The water was absolutely freezing and Jake, still holding her hand, was laughingly tugging her further into the sea, ignoring her squeals of protest. All of a sudden he had immersed them both into its salty depths and thrashing about. She found it exhilarating and endeavoured to remain in her own depth as she splashed around in a lazy attempt at the breaststroke. Jake, meanwhile, had struck out seawards in a very professional looking crawl. After a while, exhausted by her efforts, Melanie floated on her back allowing the warm rays of the sun to heat her body; her tight knot of hair had loosened due to the ducking from Jake and she let her hair float loosely about her, enjoying the feel of freedom from its elastic band.

Suddenly two masculine hands firmly gripped her waist from under the water and Melanie felt as if she had swallowed half a gallon of salt water as their grip pulled her down. Coughing and spluttering and attempting to giggle all at the same time as Jake grinned at her without any feeling of remorse. He caught her again by the hand and pulled her through the shallows and they raced up the beach. It was rather secluded along this particular stretch of sand and she supposed that they must have wandered a considerable distance around the bay; the holiday-makers could be seen a far distance away. Their bodies were shivering with their recent immersion in the cold North Sea, and, by tacit consent, return just yet to Chloe, they flung themselves, still laughing, on the fine white sand, hot to their skin. Melanie sat with her arms spread behind her in support as she leant back to allow the sun to dry her face. Water was streaming from her hair and running in tiny rivulets down her body causing her to shiver all over again.

Jake knelt behind her and gently gathered her long hair, twisted it into a coil and squeezed the excess water from it. She closed her eyes, relishing the moment of his nearness, and then suddenly flung them wide open in

surprise as she felt his warm mouth on
her bare shoulders. Slowly he turned
her to face him, looking up into his eyes
that were dark and liquid with desire;
and had she known it, her own eyes
shone with green flames, igniting a
greater response in his. Slowly, he
cupped her face between his long
capable fingers and to regain her
balance, her hands came into contact
with his wet, firm chest. She could feel
the pounding of his heart increase and
could not control her desire to spread
her fingers caressingly on his torso as he
caressed her ear, the side of her neck
and jawline, lingering with his lips.

Melanie gave herself up to the joy of
the moment, her mind closed to her
surroundings. She was only aware of his
warm, dominant mouth tracing a trail
of fire around her mouth and the heat
of his hard body so close to hers.

'I've been aching to do this for a long
time, kitten,' he murmured, before his
mouth claimed her own. Gently, he
pressed her down onto the sand until

she could feel the weight of his lean body on hers. Her mouth melted before the passionate intensity of his; she was vaguely conscious of the salty taste of the sea in their mouths. And never in her life had she been kissed in such a way. Her heart raced in time with his and by the uneven tenor of Jake's breathing, her womanly instinct registered that his self-control would soon give way; with a feeling of mild surprise she realised that she had no control over the way her body was reacting to his love-making. Suddenly Jake broke the kiss and Melanie felt abandoned. The look in her eyes must have communicated her feelings to him for he got to his knees and looked away, out to sea. 'Don't look at me like that . . . or I won't be responsible for any further actions.' His voice deep with emotion.

She blushed with shame at her wanton thoughts and, feeling deflated, got quickly to her feet, as he did, and without another word spoken, they walked apart along the sand to Chloe. This time he made no attempt to catch her hand and when she reached her beach things, Jake continued walking over to his daughter. She heard him thank the parents for looking after his child and the mother warmly replied, 'No bother at all,' and that it would have given him and his wife a nice break for half an hour.

His wife. The words dawned on Melanie's numbed brain. Chloe made matters worse by quickly correcting Mrs Allen, 'Oh no. Melanie's not my mummy. Mummy lives somewhere else, but Melanie does live with us.' Mrs Allen's smile remained on her face but she was obviously frozen with surprise, and Jake, with a wicked grin, thanked her once again but did not bother to clarify Melanie's position. Red-faced, Melanie threw a venomous glance at him as Jake dressed and, collecting the beach clutter, turned homeward for lunch.

★　★　★

As they walked up the drive a brown Ford was visible, parked outside the front door. Visitors, she thought, as she looked at Jake who was also frowning at the car. Conscious of her dishevelled appearance — her hair, although now drying must look an utter mess, hanging in dull tangles around her shoulders — Melanie's sole thought was how to get Chloe and herself up the stairs as quickly as possible to make themselves presentable for visitors. As it happened she soon forgot their untidy state when, on her entering the hall, a voice shrieked from the lounge: 'Surprise, surprise.'

She knew that voice anywhere and with a warm feeling of gratitude at her friend coming at this particular time, she rushed in to give her a friendly hug in greeting.

'We watched you coming up the drive looking like drowned rats!' Anne merrily prattled on. We . . . thought Melanie, then turning, she noticed another person. 'Why Robert, how nice of you to come all this way up here too.'

As Robert greeted her he draped his arm negligently across Anne's shoulders. At this moment Jake and Chloe came into the room and, hastily, Melanie made the necessary introductions. Jake invited them for lunch and indeed for the rest of the day and then excused himself to change for the meal. A few minutes later, Melanie and Chloe hurried upstairs to change, giggling together for no apparent reason than perhaps the advent of Anne and Robert might prove a pleasant change for the day.

* * *

The luncheon party turned out to be a jolly affair and Chloe enjoyed the company of the two guests, plying them with question after question, until finally Jake told her not to monopolize Melanie's visitors.

'What's mon-oplize?' demanded the child.

After a brief explanation from Jake, the retort from Chloe brought a quick flush to Melanie's cheeks and a very cool stare from Jake. 'You mean it's the same as when you took Melanie away on your own on the beach this morning, when I was playing with Joe and Sandy.'

Anne came to the rescue with an explanation of Robert's transfer from York. 'He got that empty flat that faces ours and guess what? He actually likes working in our office.'

'Yes . . . and if it weren't for me knocking her up every morning, neither she nor Susan would make it to work on time,' was Robert's amused comment.

'Susan?' queried Jake.

'Oh, she moved in with Anne when I came up here, Jake,' answered Melanie.

The conversation turned to their work with Jake asking various questions, and then when the guests discovered from Melanie that he had recently been in the States it was his turn to be flooded with questions. Melanie didn't contribute much to the conversation, content to listen to Jake for he was a good raconteur and was glad that he had joined them all for lunch.

Later, Melanie and Anne lounged on the terrace as they idly watched Robert instructing a grave faced Chloe on the intricacies of football. Jake had made his apologies after the lunch but he had some urgent letters to get off. It was good to see her old flatmate again and Melanie told Anne so, although making feeble excuses for the few letters she had sent her. Anne's eyes were twinkling cheekily at Melanie as she stumbled out her apologies.

'Mind you, love, you never mentioned what a dish the master of the house was. In fact, the picture you wrote of him in description was of a sour, crabby, seldom-seen mystery.'

Melanie looked down at her hands as she answered, 'Well, he can be at times.'

'You're in love with him, aren't you?'

'Yes.' Melanie's voice was almost a whisper and she knew she couldn't lie to Anne. Anne settled more comfortably in the deck chair, her long slim legs crossed and brushing her hair from her eyes, that were full of concern for her friend, she looked away to the pair playing football as she next spoke.

'I suppose he's told you he loves you too.'

Melanie threw a startled glance at her. 'Of course not. He wouldn't be interested in a nobody like myself. Anyway,' after some hesitation and in a small voice, 'anyway, even if he were, interested, I mean, it would only be a passing dalliance. He's that type of man.'

'Well you know what they say about the onlooker seeing most of the game etcetera, at lunch he struck me as being more than passingly interested in you. To tell you the truth, I got quite cross-eyed watching first him staring at you, then you back at him.'

'Oh Anne. I wasn't that obvious was

I?' wailed Melanie.

Her friend hastened to reassure her, 'No love. I know you better than most, that's all. But all the same, his glances at you didn't look platonic. Er — Melanie, there — there isn't more to tell, is there?'

Oh God, thought Melanie, if I could only put it into words. But it was too soon to speak of her emotional turbulence, and, she said as much. Anne reached for Melanie's hand and clasping it in her own for a few seconds warmly gave it a confident squeeze.

'Okay. But any difficulties and you know where to come, alright?'

'Thanks, Anne. You may be a scatterbrain but you do have some good points.' As Melanie narrowly missed a playful swipe from her scatterbrained friend, 'Anyway,' she continued on a lighter note, 'enough of this maudlin conversation, now what about our friend Robert?' Melanie stabbed an accusing finger at Anne. 'Never even a mention of him moving up to Durham.'

'I've been saving that piece of news as a surprise. And I wanted to come up here without letting you know as an even bigger surprise.' Anne's smile faded. 'Alright, I'll be serious for once, if I can. I think he's terrific, Robert, I mean. In fact I'm crazy about him and my feelings are definitely reciprocated but Robert thinks as we have only known each other a short time . . . ' Anne spread her hands and shrugged, 'He's a bit on the cautious side, but don't worry, I bet we're engaged before Christmas.'

Melanie looked at her friend, then at Robert out on the lawn, and after a brief pause, 'I think I can give my approval on him. You may continue with this romance.' Throwing a sly wink at Anne.

'And would you like my seal of approval on Jake Masters?'

'Oh shut up.' Melanie quickly got to her feet and tipped Anne, playfully, from her deck chair. 'Come on, let's join in the football.'

Later Melanie noticed Rose setting the table for tea out on the terrace and thought it only good manners to assist her as Anne and Robert were really her guests. Excusing herself from the others, she entered the house intent on going first upstairs to wash. With this purpose in mind — to be as quick as she could — she collided into a masculine sweater-clad chest at the head of the stairs. Strong arms steadied her impact and, for an instant, it was a pleasure to remain in their heady haven. Jake must have thought so too for he also seemed as reluctant to release her.

'What's the rush, kitten?' he drawled, his breath warm on her cheek as he looked down at her.

She struggled in his arms until he abruptly released her; Melanie stammered an apology and moved towards the bathroom. Why did he always reduce her to the state of a confused, inadequate schoolgirl? She had really wanted to draw that proud arrogant head down to her own and let him wreak havoc on her mouth with his own. Her stomach churned nervously in the remembrance of his love-making this morning. And then inwardly she despised herself for her feelings towards a man that was not the person for her.

On the way back down the stairs, the shrill note of the phone in the hall interrupted her troubled thoughts. She picked up the receiver and automatically gave the home number.

'Who's that?' was the sharp feminine voice in an American accent.

'Who do you wish to speak to?' was Melanie's brief counter-question. After a short breathless pause, the American voice asked for Jake.

She moved into the kitchen to help with the tea as she called Jake from the garden where he had joined in the game of football. Nobody in the kitchen could have failed to hear Jake's part in the telephone call so Melanie, being the sole occupant of that room, unashamedly listened on.

'Why, Julia, honey, this is a surprise . . . when did you fly in? ' A brief pause when Melanie could almost hear that sharp American voice literally gabbling on the other end of the line. 'Well I don't think I'll be able to make it, honey. Where's that devoted husband of yours? . . . Oh . . . I see . . . where are you staying? . . . The Savoy, er . . . maybe. Who?' A short laugh from Jake. 'Would you believe me if I said the maid.'

American voice had been asking who she was. She arranged the tiny sandwiches on the plate three times, straining to hear more of the conversation, but at that moment Rose bustled in; Melanie had no choice but to take the food out to the terrace. Hot stabs of jealousy pricked in the region of her heart and she hated Jake: just then for the way he was fooling about with her emotions, and despised him for his expertise on handling women. He was a married man yet making passes at herself, and now this Julia person; who, judging by the overheard phone call, was also married, and he had certainly been having an affair with her at some time.

The tea table was arranged and this time Anne took Chloe into the house to wash their grubby hands. With a bright smile on her face, Melanie indicated to Robert the way to the cloakroom to freshen up although inwardly she felt utterly miserable. She sighed — it had been a lovely day until that phone call — as she waited for the others to rejoin her. The sun still shone, bright and hot in the garden that was a joy to behold; her dear friend had come up all the way from Durham to see her. She experienced a sudden rage at Jake: it was all his fault. He thinks I'm his for the asking; well, that's all he thinks, she mused, as a seed of an idea began to germinate in her mind.

The man of her thoughts was the first to appear and with a saccharin sweet smile she looked up at him as he stood by her chair. Indeed the smile seemed to be having no mean effect on him as he idly flicked her long hair from her cheek. Returning her smile as he noted that her friends' visit seemed to have done her good as she had been looking a little peaked lately. At that moment the others trooped out and joined them at the table. After everyone was seated and Melanie began to pour tea she idly asked Anne, 'How's Matthew these days?'

At first Anne did not answer immediately, her gaze narrowed at the question. What was Melanie's game now? she thought with some foreboding. She knew that look on Melanie's face. She was brewing up trouble if she was correct in thinking that she was trying to make Jake jealous for some obscure reason. Matthew had been one of Melanie's boyfriends until she had come up here.

'Matthew's fine . . . he asked me for your address but that's up to you . . . if you want to write to him . . . ' Anne shrugged, dismissing the subject.

During this discussion, Chloe had

been talking to her father about their game of football. He was looking at his daughter but his mind was on the conversation of the others. His face was immobile, not showing any sign of displeasure, but he turned an enigmatic stare at Melanie as she replied, 'Actually, I'll wait and see him when I drive down home, on a weekend off.' There, it was said and maybe now Jake will discard any ideas of her 'infatuation' with him.

By the warning looks from Anne to Melanie, it only proved she didn't like this conversation at all, and after tea she took Melanie up to her bedroom to tidy herself before going home. She scolded Melanie fiercely for her tactics. Her grey eyes were wide and cloudy with concern as she flicked a brush jerkily through her flyaway hair. She stared at her friend's reflection through the vanity mirror and clicked her tongue in beration. 'What was that idea about Matthew? It's no good playing that sort of game with a man like Jake, you silly goose.'

'Don't worry, I'll explain it all when I get a weekend off. I merely wanted to let the man know I wasn't that serious about him . . . anyway, I think it worked.'

'Worked . . . I could see Jake getting furious, he hardly said a word for the rest of the meal. It was a silly, childish idea,' Anne ended emphatically.

After her visitors had gone, the evening seemed a little flat. Chloe, tired after her romp in the garden, willingly went to bed as Rose ushered her up the stairs after wishing Melanie 'good-night'. Jake had disappeared ages ago back to his study. Melanie decided to go for a stroll down to the beach; the air was oppressive after the hot day and the low, ominous rumblings in the far distant hills heralded a possible thunderstorm later in the night. Everywhere was still; for once there was no breeze whispering relentlessly through the long grass on the dunes. Even the sea was calm, turning its waves lazily and with effort up the beach. The quiet was relaxing and the cool, damp sand made a splatting noise beneath her bare feet, sandals in her hands, as she pattered along the shoreline. Presently she made her way up towards the dunes and sat down in a small hollow, enjoying one of her rare cigarettes. The sand was still warm to the touch and, although early evening, comfortable to sit down on.

Large, slow splashes of rain on her face and bare arms woke Melanie to the realization that she must have drifted off to sleep lying on the warm sand. The light had almost gone from the sky and if she didn't hurry back she would be in for a soaking. A bright flash of blue lightening flickered across the sky, illuminating the beach in an eerie light for an instant, as Melanie scrambled over the dunes on her hasty way home. As she reached the door, a loud crash of thunder reverberated around her and, with a satisfied sigh and a pause to regain her breath, she knew she had gained cover just in time.

As she reached for the inner door handle, it gave inwards at the same time, to reveal Jake standing there looking at her in such a hostile manner that it caused Melanie's temper to rise in self-defence, as he frowned down at her.

'Where the hell have you been all this time?' was his irate greeting.

Melanie stormed past him into the kitchen to make a hot drink, refusing to answer his rude tirade. She was in the act of reaching in one of the top cupboards for the coffee, when a large brown hand covered the door she was trying to open.

'I asked where you had been. You could have been drenched out in that, I was just about to come and look for you.' His voice had softened, so his temper must have simmered down a little, she mused.

The rain was coming down in torrents, straight from the heavens and making loud echoing splashes in the courtyard as she glanced at the kitchen window. Whether it was the look of all the rain or the nearness of Jake, standing right behind her that made her shiver, she could not tell.

'I just went for a stroll on the beach and fell asleep, no crime in that, surely?'

Slowly he turned her to face him, his hands softly holding her shoulders and Melanie felt herself holding her breath in panic at the feel of his fingers softly pressing on her bare arms.

'Why? To think about this Matthew person or — perhaps to think about what happened between us on the beach this morning, hmm?' His voice was softly insistent and probing, like his fingers now moving up to the hollows of her shoulders. She raised her eyes helplessly to meet his and for an instant she thought he had a tortured look in his eyes, his scar was vividly whiter on his tanned face and his dark eyes troubled and concerned as he looked at her.

Only for an instant, then Melanie's lips curled in derision as she recollected the phone call to Julia, and onto his wife living somewhere away from him, perhaps of his womanizing. Still she did not say anything and his voice became thicker at his next question.

'Didn't it mean anything to you at all? Don't deny it, I could have taken you then and there on the beach.'

Her face burned with his meaning and anger at herself and at him for his persuasive talk flared and erupted as she shrugged his hands from her. 'Haven't you heard of physical attraction? a romp in the sea; a run across the sands; a man and a woman . . . the kiss was inevitable.' Melanie even managed to give a short laugh which sounded cracked in her own ears. 'It was nice while it lasted, but that's it. You're making a big issue out of nothing.'

There was a short ominous silence, then with deliberate and cruel movements, he caught her by the shoulders.

'You're a little bitch, I was right the first time I saw you in that bar, and I'm no boy like your Matthew to be played around with . . . I can play any game with you . . . darling,' he ground the endearment out in an insulting way as he savagely took her mouth in total possession with his own.

Melanie struggled vainly, for his hands held her in a vice-like grip. Her own hands were caught between their bodies. Flames of response were flowing like wildfire through her veins until she could fight no longer and instead relaxed her body against his. That caused Jake to raise his mouth above hers for a second as he looked triumphantly in her eyes before he took her mouth again in a groan of despair. Her arms wound themselves round his neck to curl her fingers in his hair at the back of his neck, and he held her body all the more tightly against his own hard form. She uttered a shuddering sigh of pleasure as his hands moved down her body, caressing her small firm breasts, then round to the small of her back to press her more closely to his hard, muscular thighs. She could have remained there forever in this vortex of sensation within the circle of his arms, feeling the rapidly increasing beats of his heart intermingled with her own; his warm, hard body pressing desirously closer to hers; his mouth moving over her face and neck and then irresistably back to her mouth, opening willingly to his own, as he muttered thickly, 'Oh God, how I've wanted you, I can hardly keep away from you, damn you, woman.'

The words seemed forced from him but Melanie wanted only his arms, his mouth and his body at this moment. The sounds of the rain drumming on the windows her ears ringing with her own heavy heartbeats . . . until she realized the ringing was the drum of the telephone in the hall. Still Jake did not release her. Perhaps he had not heard, intent in pursuing the passion between them. But the voice of Rose Kennedy as she answered the call must have picked its way through to his thoughts for she was so abruptly let go that she fell against the cupboards. Just at that moment the kitchen door opened and the housekeeper looked at them both long and searchingly, before she mentioned that the call was for Jake.

He tore his gaze from Melanie and raked a hand through his dishevelled hair then strode without a word to either of the women out of the room. Melanie's eyes lowered before the piercing scrutiny of the housekeeper's, conscious of her ruffled clothing and naked, bruised mouth, still tingling from the pressure of Jake's kisses. She muttered an inaudible goodnight to the woman and almost ran out of the room to the sanctuary of her bedroom. The voice of Jake followed her up the stairs.

'Yes, Julia. I think I'll be able to manage it after all, darling . . . don't be impatient, I'll ring you as soon as I get to London.'

4

It was Saturday evening, the day before Chloe's birthday, and Melanie and Rose were relaxing in the lounge. The television film was an old western and Rose was watching it avidly. Melanie had a magazine on her lap, trying to interest herself in the print, but she found it hard work trying to concentrate with the volume on the set rather loud.

'I'll just turn it down a little, Rose. The noise might waken Chloe.' Then, turning to the housekeeper: 'Is that alright? Can you hear okay?'

Rose waved a languid hand in mid-air, anxious for Melanie to remove her person from her line of vision. 'Oh, I'm sorry. Yes. Fine, thanks.' Melanie gave up the idea of reading the book and, tucking her bare feet under the long folds of her green cotton kaftan, she resigned herself to watching the end of the film. But she couldn't concentrate and her thoughts centred on the person who had not been seen by the household for a week.

Jake had left for London very early the morning after Rose had interrupted their passionate scene together in the kitchen. Nobody, not even the housekeeper, had seen him depart, although he had notified her of his intentions after Julia Marwood had telephoned. Melanie knew that Rose was only being kindly and thinking of her interest when she had gone into great detail about Jake's absorption with Julia Marwood. Everything was told to her, but to hear a third party endorsing and clarifying a situation that she already had deliberated, turned knife wounds in her heart.

Julia and Jake had enjoyed a tempestuous affair while they were all living in the States. The American woman's marriage was only a few months old to a famous financier when their affair started. Jake, as usual, cared little for convention, nor whether Julia wanted their 'association' made public or not. Rose was relieved when she noticed Jake beginning to tire of Julia for soon after that, she had made a dramatic reconciliation with her husband. Not before many tongues had wagged maliciously, for it was rumoured that her husband had stated to the press that he was seeking a divorce. No more had been heard of Julia until the phone call recently. At the time Jake had been totally unaffected by the whole business and was soon escorting a well-known top model after the scandal had erupted. Perhaps Rose wanted to impress on her, Melanie, the futility of harbouring any future hopes of Jake's attraction for her and so she continued relentlessly, describing the past women in his life, all of them of the same calibre: hard and calculating as they were beautiful, but well able to look after themselves in any situation. When the affairs had ended, the pattern was always the same: endless phone calls until, finally, Jake would instruct

Rose to say the inevitable: 'Away on business.'

'He's not the man for you, dear,' she advised Melanie quietly, 'please take heed of all I've said. He'll wear your emotions into tatters. Jake is too experienced and cynical for you.'

'Then why have you stayed with him . . . if he's such a pig?' She regretted the churlish words immediately but the housekeeper understood the bitter retort.

'No dear. You see I really blame his wife for his attitude towards women. He idolized Marion but she threw it all back in his face. She tired of the marriage pretty soon and then, well, when the child was expected . . . dear me, she was furious. Blamed him. The quarrels were terrible. She was a bitch, make no mistake. All she worried about was the state of her thickening figure and her dancing career.' Her voice became harsh and bitter at her memories. 'Jake had to watch her like a hawk for even I heard her threaten to get rid of the baby . . . I knew she'd leave him. Good riddance to her, I said to myself at the time. Chloe was only a month old. Anyway after that, he started having affair after affair. So now you know.' There was silence after that for a while and then Rose finished warningly, 'Remember, Melanie, he only wants women for his own necessary purposes . . . I don't have to spell those out for you, do I?'

★　★　★

Melanie's eyes focussed, blinking rapidly; the television was playing to an unresponsive audience. Rose was dozing opposite her, the film having ended and a chat show in progress. She sighed against the weight of her entangled problems. Perhaps the best thing would be to hand in her notice and run back to Durham, forget him as quickly as possible. There again, to stay and be disillusioned would be a more painful remedy but effective. And always lurking in the far corners of her mind, the faint hope that he could come to really love her as she knew she loved him, with or without his faults.

Sounds from the other sofa proved to be the housekeeper waking up and murmuring something about a light snack for them both, as she tried to stifle the yawn at the same time.

'I'll make something for a change,' as Melanie as she hastily got to her feet, relieved to do something physical rather than to sit and brood. 'You sit there and watch the show.' The older woman made half-hearted protests but Melanie could see she was happy to relax a little longer and have the luxury of being waited on for a change. As she prepared the tray of appetizing toasted sandwiches in the kitchen she espied the birthday cake for Chloe in the larder, the final decorating touches made by the housekeeper earlier that day. Jake had never discussed the proposed picnic with her, as he had promised. Never mind, she was determined that there would be an outing, with or without her father.

*　*　*

Replete after their snack, Melanie fell into a fitful doze as she patiently sat with the other woman to watch the midnight movie. Rose had hinted that it was a spine chiller and would not have dared to watch it if Melanie had not been with her. It didn't prove to be full of that much suspense for Melanie fell asleep after a few minutes: her hair falling in a dark curtain over one side of her face as she snuggled into the cushion: her graceful form incumbent along the sofa.

So it was that she didn't hear Rose's exclamation of surprise as the reflection of a car's headlights lit up the lounge as it swung past the window around to the back of the house. Still she did not stir as the housekeeper hurried out into the hall.

'Jake?' she murmured in a soft

questioning voice as footsteps sounded at the front porch.

The mumble of voices in the hall registered vaguely in the far regions of Melanie's sleep-fuddled mind, slowly rousing her to consciousness. She sensed rather than heard someone walking into the room then stand, watching her, as she opened her eyes to see Jake looking down at her, his face impassive. For several seconds neither moved nor spoke, green eyes locked with grey as if in unspoken battle, then, warily, she tried to sit up in a graceful position on the sofa.

'I, er, hope you had a good journey back . . . you must be tired.'

'Tired?'

'The journey . . . it's . . . it's a long way.' She could sense the tension starting to build up between them, almost a tangible thing, Oh God, he might be a bit more pleasant.

Jake ran his hand through his hair at the back of his neck — a nervous gesture? — but no, she repudiated this thought immediately.

'Er, Mrs Kennedy . . . does she know you've arrived?'

He sat down on the sofa and turned his long, lithe body towards her, his arm draped casually along the back. She only had to lean over and raise her hand to cover his, large and brown against the cream leather. She resisted this impulsive action so much it was almost painful.

'How are things?' His voice was deep and husky dispelling her frivolous thoughts concerning him.

'Oh, just fine. Mrs Kennedy's made Chloe a beautiful cake for tomorrow'.

At this juncture, in walked the housekeeper carrying a laden tray of sandwiches and coffee. The conversation was a bit easier with a third party and talk was general. Perhaps the older woman had sensed the strained atmosphere and was doing her best to relieve it. Eventually Jake relaxed and helped himself to the food prepared, answering questions about London. Melanie said very little, and looking closely at Jake she thought he looked very tired. Lines of weariness, that she had not noticed before on his face, etched deeply around his eyes; it made him look older yet more vulnerable.

Tired herself, Melanie stifled a yawn and received a glimmer of a smile from Jake as he noticed the action. She got to her feet murmuring that she was off to bed when Jake interrupted with the proposed outing on Chloe's birthday, tomorrow. Quite casually he instructed the housekeeper that they would all leave in the morning for a drive towards the borders, and perhaps return around tea-time. He hoped that these arrangements would suit, he finished in an arrogant tone. Rose declined to accompany them as she would like to prepare some delicacies for the tea table, however she wished the rest of them an enjoyable day. Melanie felt slightly nervous at the thoughts of his company for several hours but pushed these ideas at the back of her mind. She decided, after all, it was Chloe's birthday and she, Melanie, was determined that the little girl would enjoy herself.

The next morning, Melanie was almost first downstairs, and hearing someone in the dining room and the clatter of crockery, she pushed open the door.

'Morning, Melanie, oh, what a lovely dress. Yes,' the housekeeper stood back a little as she stared at the figure, 'yes, it suits you very well.' She had dressed with especial care today, her hair bright and shining, twisted in its usual coil on her head, accentuating her slender neck. The fine lawn of her green dress, falling in soft feminine folds to her knees, and matching high-heeled sandals completed the outfit. She placed her gayly packaged gift at Chloe's setting on the table. At that moment, Jake and his daughter came into the room and everyone wished her a 'very happy birthday' as she ran to them all with hugs and kisses. Her small, brown face was beaming with excitement, as any child's would be when a birthday came around. Unobtrusively, two small packages had also been placed on the table as they took their places. They all watched Chloe indulgently as she undid the presents.

Melanie sipped her orange juice as Jake fastened the beautiful silver watch on his daughter's wrist, Chloe was absolutely delighted with this very grown up present. Jake, as well as Melanie, had dressed with care this morning. The dark suit and cream shirt, with navy striped tie was very elegant and masculine; his hair, she noticed, was still damp from his recent shower. She looked back to Chloe, who was admiring Auntie Rose's present, fastened on her other wrist: a fine silver bracelet. Melanie's painting set was equally on show on the table. The child thanked them all very prettily for her delightful presents.

After breakfast, they all assembled for the outing, Melanie ran upstairs for a forgotten handkerchief and when she appeared at the car outside, she found Chloe and Jake already in the car. With surprise she noted that the child was in the rear; hesitantly she opened the front passenger door that Jake indicated and looked over to Chloe enquiringly.

'Daddy spun a coin to see who was sitting where first.' Chloe must have been able to understand Melanie's silent question. 'I don't mind sitting in the back, 'cos I'll be able to change over coming back.'

All Melanie received from Jake was an enigmatic glance and then he released the clutch and with a wave at the waiting housekeeper they were cruising along the drive to the open road.

They were travelling along the coast road. Melanie looked over her shoulder at Chloe, who returned the smile, and then, as she turned to look out of the front window, her smile turned to a grimace of horror. Melanie's brain froze at the sight of the oncoming car, careering wildly from one side of the road to the other. She faintly heard Jake's cry of 'Bloody idiot', then it was nearly upon them. She was aware of the quick, decisive action of Jake as he swerved to avoid a crash, the sound of screaming tyres . . . and the impact was avoided. Her eyes were screwed tight together in a momentary reflex action and, as Jake tried to regain control of their car, it lurched and dipped in an unbalacing motion, knocking her to-wards the side door. And then blackness descended, blocking out the terrified moments.

The first thing Melanie was aware of was the physical sensation of floating. It was rather pleasant until a stabbing pain in her head began to take effect. She opened her eyes to find herself being carried in Jake's arms, her head nestling in the fine material of his dark jacket, against his chest. She stirred, and Jake looked down at her, his face white beneath the tan. She guessed with surprise that he looked worried and anxious as she moaned faintly with the painful throbbing in her head.

'Hush, you're alright, just a bit bruised and shaken.' As reaction set in and Melanie began to tremble uncontrollably, the silent tears squeezing out of tightly closed lids.

He must have been carrying her up the stairs, for the next flash of consciousness was of being lowered gently onto her bed. opening her eyes she recognized the furnishings of her own bedroom. Jake's face was very close to her own and the worried expression in his eyes was a new experience from his usual arrogant or sensual stare. Perhaps the sympathetic glance — Melanie was too confused to think clearly, caused the tears to start afresh. She closed her eyes again to try to stem the flow. Gently a large, brown hand wiped away her distress and she felt herself drift away into blessed oblivion.

★   ★   ★

She awoke to find it was evening, late evening, she surmised; the curtains were drawn to shut out the night. At first she was content to lie prostrate underneath the bedclothes until memory returned and she recollected the near crash. Although why had she ended up hurt? The other car hadn't hit them and then she remembered the lurching motion and her body reeling against the side door. The pain in her head didn't seem so bad as before and when she raised a hand to tentatively probe the damage she winced at the feeling of a lump at the side of her brow. She needed to inspect the damage and, shakily tossing the bedcovers aside, she groped her way to the dressing mirror.

'Beautiful,' was her verdict as she looked at the elaborate bruising and feebly laughed at her reflection, although wincing at the movement. There was an immediate knock on the door and even before she answered the door swung open to reveal Jake standing there.

'What the hell are you doing out of bed?' The admonition was softened by the low, tender note in his voice, as he stood uncertain in the doorway.

Conscious of her near nakedness, for she was dressed in a long, palest pink, nylon nightie — she supposed Rose had dressed her for bed — she noticed the diaphonous attire was having its effect on Jake as his eyes caressed the length of her body. Heat suffused her skin, from head to toes, and suddenly he moved quickly towards her and before she realized his intent, he had lifted her back onto the bed. She was very much aware of his warm hands touching her as he held her light form and she knew by the tightening of his jaw that he was not unaffected by his action.

'What happened?' croaked Melanie, when she had managed to find her voice at last.

Jake finished straightening the bed-clothes and stood by the door, as if in haste to be out of the room. His eyes looked dark and full of concern, eyes that could look so cool and icy at times.

'I'll tell you in the morning. You were the only one hurt and I don't think you were aware that the doc's been to examine you. Shocked and bruised, was his diagnosis, and you're to spend a couple of days in bed. So . . . get to sleep, see you tomorrow.'

'Goodnight then, Jake.' Her eyes felt heavy, perhaps she had been given a sedative without her knowing.

'Night, kitten,' as he softly closed the door behind him.

★   ★   ★

The weather was dull and miserable, reflecting her own thoughts and state as she lay back on the pillows and stared out of the window. Her head did not ache so badly as the previous evening but she was very much aware of the livid bruising on her brow. Poor Chloe, what a birthday treat it had turned out to be. Her gaze wandered from the grey tightly packed clouds scudding across the sky out of the window to around her room and finally to settle in curious detachment on the pale pink roses, delicately arranged by the housekeeper and placed on the dressing unit shelf.

The bouquet had arrived early that morning and the enclosed card had merely read: *Get well soon — Simon Armstrong*, written in a very flowery, artistic hand.

Jake hadn't seemed too pleased about the idea of this Simon sending her a bouquet. Paying her a visit after breakfast, he had frowned as he read the card near the vase.

'I gather from Mrs Kennedy that this man,' as she indicated the flowers, 'er, that this man was the other driver.'

'Mmm.' Jake stared at the flowers, so perfect in their long-stemmed beauty, as if they were a particularly nasty type of weed.

'We-ell?' Honestly, was he ever going to tell her the incident?

And so Jake related how Simon's tyre had burst and as he had been driving at considerable speed, he had lost control of his car. That was when they had been driving along and he, Jake, had just had time to swerve and avoid the impact when they had run into a ditch. Melanie had banged her head against the side window, hence her injuries. No one else had suffered any injuries, least of all Simon Armstrong, who had managed to bring his car to a halt not very farther up the road. He and Jake had halted an oncoming car and they had brought her straight back here. Later, they had gone back to their cars and sorted things out, investigating damages and so on.

A light tap at the bedroom door revealed Rose who seemed somewhat taken aback to find Jake in the room. She said nothing, merely raised an eyebrow in Melanie's direction as Jake, back towards them, was looking out of the window.

'Simon Armstrong's here to see how you are, Melanie.'

Jake turned suddenly from the window. 'She's not well enough to see any visitors.' He hadn't even given Melanie the chance to speak and she thought his excuse ludicrous after all: Jake was here, wasn't he? There again she did not want to see any strangers, she certainly wasn't up to making social conversation. Well, perhaps she felt a small twinge of disappointment not to see this mysterious Simon, who had sent her the extravagant flowers.

'I'll have a word with him.' Jake left the room with the housekeeper.

In the afternoon, Chloe crept in, looking very secretive and she explained to a puzzled-looking Melanie that she 'had orders not to disturb her' but couldn't resist a small 'peek at the invalid'. Honestly, Jake was the limit at times: invalid indeed. Still, Melanie was getting a little bored lying around, and was pleased to see Chloe who had jumped onto the bed clutching the rag doll that Melanie had brought her when she first arrived to take up her post.

Swinging her legs, she grinned at the girl in the bed.

'What a beautiful bump, it's horrible and gory looking.' With her usual childlike tact she had wiped out any morale Melanie had left. 'You should've seen the way Daddy went on when he saw you lying all slumped and dead looking. He was furious with that Simon man.' Chloe's eyes grew larger in dramatic effect. 'I thought he'd kill him . . . he looked so mad.'

Melanie was rather intrigued to find this out and couldn't resist trying to get some more information from the unsuspecting child.

'What's this Simon man like, then?'

Chloe had jumped off the bed to wander round the room, she gave an adult shrug at the question, 'Oh . . . not as old as Daddy, not young though, but of course Daddy's ancient so . . . he asked me if I was alright and came here this morning to see you . . . Daddy saw him . . . he said he'd be back tomorrow.'

* ★ ★ ★

Melanie did indeed meet Simon the next morning. She had refused to stay in bed and Jake had conceded to her to come downstairs but not to go gallivanting off to the beach. She was in the lounge when Rose ushered Simon Armstrong in to meet her. She was glad that she had arranged her hair to fall over the bruising on her brow and thus conceal the unsightly colouring. Simon turned out to be an entertaining visitor; after apologizing for the accident, he soon put her at her ease and she was surprised to hear that he and Jake knew each other quite well. They had spent their boyhood together and had been to the same public school. Simon's home was further up the coast. The thought came to her that it was strange that Jake had not said any of this; in fact, he had given the impression that this man was a stranger.

Simon, and they were instantly on first name terms, had been working abroad for the last few years, which accounted for his deep tan. Melanie was not unaffected by his natural charm and she considered him extremely handsome as she studied his face whilst he chattered on about his work in South America. Tall and lean with light hair that had been bleached ash blonde in the Brazilian sun, his eyes were clear sunshine blue and at the moment he was gazing at Melanie with masculine interest.

She felt completely at ease with him, he had that kind of personality, and in no time he had her giggling helplessly at his description of Jake's wrath at the 'scene of the crime'. She felt a little guilty to laugh at Jake but Simon's account was too amusing. Her giggles quickly subsided as she met the cold eyes of the very person of their entertainment. Goodness, how long had he been standing there in the doorway? She felt her cheeks redden in embarrassment and judging by the austere expression on his face he must have heard something of their conversation not to his liking. Jake greeted Simon amiably enough and Melanie offered him a cup of coffee. As he turned his back on Simon to accept it from her, she intercepted a slow, meaningful wink from Simon that caused a glimmer of a smile on her lips.

'I've been trying to persuade Melanie to have dinner with me this Saturday. Doesn't she get any time off from you Jake, you old slavedriver?'

'She only has to ask.' Jake's look was piercing at Melanie.

She could have thrown the contents of her cup at Simon's grinning face, not sure how to take this unexpected invitation. She was annoyed with him at having lied to Jake, for no such question had been put to her, and at the same time, the company of an unattached, attractive male would make a nice change and put her own problems at the back of her mind for a while. Perhaps it would put her feelings for

Jake into a clearer perspective.

'Well I don't . . . '

Simon interrupted Melanie's uncertain speech. 'That settles it. I'll call for you at seven on Saturday and put your prettiest dress on, although you would look gorgeous in a sack to me.'

Not long after, he made his farewells, and Melanie was thankful in all honesty that he had departed, for it was markedly noticeable that with Jake's presence an atmosphere had settled in the lounge. Jake, however, seemed in no hurry to vacate the room, and he settled on the sofa, absorbed in the morning newspaper. She attempted some form of idle conversation but got such uncompromising short replies from him that she soon gave up the idea. To give herself something to do other than stare around the room trying to avoid looking at him she flicked idly through a fashion magazine, not able to read anything, too keyed up to concentrate. When she suddenly looked up to steal a glance at his face, her heart nearly missed a beat to find Jake staring at her with a thoughtful expression on his rugged face.

'I want to give you a word of warning . . . ' He hesitated as she looked back at him in blank surprise, 'Simon Armstrong has been known to have broken several hearts in the past. I don't want you getting too involved with a man like that okay?'

Well of all the cheek! Melanie didn't like this kind of advice one little bit. His attitude of the heavy father act was a bit much. Indeed, he hadn't been exactly platonic with his relationship with herself recently. She was amazed at his blunt warning and in any case, nobody, least of all Melanie, liked being told what and what not to do with her personal life. He had no right, no right at all. Indignation rose up in her throat at the very thought of it. She flung the magazine down, a mutinous expression tightening her mouth. 'I'm only having dinner with the man. What's all the fuss for heaven's sake?'

Jake seemed about to elucidate further when Chloe came bursting into the room. A very grubby looking Chloe, who had been assisting old Mason out in the garden this morning. Melanie hurried the child upstairs on Jake's disapproving look at his daughter's filthy appearance, to get cleaned up before lunch. She regretted that Jake had been unable to continue the conversation; it might have proven very interesting and the sneaking thought at the back of her mind was that Jake's special concern might be through plain jealousy. If only it were true, Melanie would have been delighted if it were.

* * *

She could hear Simon's voice in the hall downstairs that heralded his arrival as she put the finishing touches to her appearance. A few sprays of her precious French perfume and she picked up the fine woollen shawl from the bed. She gave a last look at her appearance in the mirror and surveyed herself with satisfaction. Dressing up certainly improved a girl's morale, she told her reflection in the long dusky pink halter neck dress. Her hair she had left hanging down her bare shoulders, a curtain of fine black silk against her skin as it swung about her when she moved. A last application of matching pink lipstick that accentuated the golden tan and she walked elegantly down the stairs, thankful that careful make-up had effectively hidden the near fading bruise on her brow.

The fact that Jake was nowhere to be seen was a disappointment to her, for she would have liked his approving look on her appearance. Instead Simon showed his appreciation by the long low whistle he gave her as he watched her descent. Rose came out of the kitchen and added her approval by commenting on the beautiful dress and, as she wished them a nice evening, she pressed a key into Melanie's hand as Simon waited for Melanie to precede him from the house.

The hotel was about half an hour's journey and they decided to have a drink in the cocktail bar before claiming the table Simon had reserved for their meal. Melanie was determined to enjoy herself and found it an easy exercise for she knew Simon would be an interesting companion. Although she was not deceived by his practised charm, and realized Jake would have been right; for Simon's handsome looks would turn many a woman's head and in fact several feminine glances had turned his way already in the crowded bar.

She thought the meal super, never before having had the means to dine in such extravagant splendour. The lobster thermidor lived up to her expectations as did the rest of the courses. Simon talked incessantly throughout the meal, about his parents who owned a considerable estate in the county, his father still taking a keen interest in farming. Simon had been a disappointment for he had never had any leanings towards agricultural activities and had followed a career as a civil engineer working mainly abroad. He had a sister, Sonia, who was a journalist, a very successful one at that, and she was in Paris on an assignment at the present, but Melanie was sure to meet her shortly for she was due home next week.

'Once she knows that Jake's back in circulation here, then she'll be around,' he admitted wryly.

Melanie felt a bit apprehensive at his warning tone but said no more to draw the subject of his sister into the conversation. Most of Simon's chatter went above Melanie's head and she was quite content to enjoy the meal, their surroundings and the music of the small orchestra playing in a corner of the room. Simon, noticing her look at the musicians, asked her to dance, and they did so frequently between courses. He was a perfect dancer and to

Melanie's rusty steps of modern dancing he was a good partner. Perhaps he did hold her a fraction too tightly, and the fact that Melanie couldn't help imagining that it was Jake's arms around her some of the time made her relax against him, engrossed in those thoughts. Simon's reaction was all male and he would hold her even tighter and once his mouth brushed her earlobe lightly and caused her to draw back in dismay.

They drank champagne throughout the evening and later Melanie felt quite light-headed and refused to have any more to drink. Simon was adamant and would refill her glass until finally she pretended to sip the wine. Eventually, the dancing ended about two in the morning and she thought with surprise how quickly her evening had passed as Simon drove slowly homewards. At the door Melanie thanked him for a wonderful evening and his answer was to draw her slowly into his arms and gently caress her lips with his own. She didn't resist for he was a very attractive male, and when his kiss deepened, for a second she responded, thoughts always of Jake at the back of her mind and how his lovemaking would affect her. Then she despised herself for using such a nice person as Simon in this way and broke the embrace.

'Oh no . . . I can't find the key,' she moaned as she fumbled in her bag.

They searched for several minutes in her bag, then back in the car in case it had dropped on the floor, but to no avail. Walking back to the front porch, Simon muttered something about shinning up a drainpipe to her room that reduced them both to giggles again. Suddenly the steps were lit up with an inside light turned on and the door opened as Simon grabbed a surprised Melanie and kissed her hard on the mouth. She stood quiescent in his arms, so taken aback at his action.

'Goodnight, darling Melanie, I'll ring you tomorrow.' Simon breathed the words against her mouth and, sketching a salute at a glowering Jake in the doorway, he turned towards his car.

Melanie stood in a welter of confusion. She couldn't see Jake's face properly for he stood with his back to the light from the doorway but she could sense his disapproval all the same. He stood back to allow her to step inside and Melanie stammered out an apology for losing the key. Jake merely looked at her as if the subject bored him.

'I was on my way to bed and heard you outside.' His voice, full of censure like a Victorian father, made her giggle and then wish she hadn't. 'Very beautiful . . . was all this for Simon's benefit?' Soft were his words that transmitted warning tingles of awareness through the length of her body. They were standing very close in the hall, and he moved closer to lift the fallen shawl from one shoulder back in its place; his fingers trailing like firebrands on her naked skin.

'Did Simon give you a good time?'

'Yes thanks.' She couldn't think of any other answer rather than a trite reply.

'I noticed you disregarded my warning.'

She frowned at the question unable to comprehend his meaning.

'If his parting goodnight kiss is anything to go by.' He said the words almost through closed teeth.

Suddenly bitterness against this man rose up in her, his attraction was deadly and she could stand no more of his baiting. 'And why not? you taught me to enjoy kisses like that.' The words were almost hissed back at him.

Jake's hand went involuntarily round the back of her neck to twist her hair in an agonizing coil, pulling her close to his body, her eyes wide in anger, flashing green fire in resentment of his violent action. His nostrils flared, in like anger, but his eyes darkened at her nearness, even in anger, their bodies treacherously aware of each other. With a groan he released her and Melanie felt a flame of triumph at her power over him.

'Goodnight, Jake.' And she walked up the stairs, strangely elated.

As she prepared for bed she thought of Simon and felt ashamed. She resolved not to go out with the man again, for it was unfair to play off one man against the other, and if she were honest, hadn't that been the real reason for her date tonight? Her feminine instincts told her that her plan had certainly succeeded but she felt disgusted with herself for all that.

5

Surprisingly, Melanie fell into a deep sleep, to wake much refreshed the following morning. Her light-hearted manner seemed to infect the rest of the household; Rose was actually whistling softly as she prepared breakfast. When Melanie returned from the garden with Chloe, Jake was about in the kitchen. The talk was desultory around the breakfast table and then, on impulse, Melanie asked Jake if she might take Chloe for a ride to Durham, to visit Anne. She surprised herself as well as everyone else with her request. Chloe received the news ecstatically, and enthusiasm overtook her tongue by asking if her father would also join them which rather threw Melanie off balance, mentally. She held her breath and then was delighted to hear his reply.

'Sure . . . why not?' He looked at Melanie, defying her to contradict him.

The sky was downcast but it didn't seem to dampen anybody's spirits as they headed south in the opulent Jensen.

'You know, it's funny Jake, but . . . I had decided to take Chloe on this trip for her birthday . . . that is if you hadn't returned home.' She turned to his daughter, wriggling about impatiently on the back seat, eager to reach their destination. 'Anyway, Chloe, regard this as your belated birthday outing, hmm?'

Melanie still had her key to the flat but instead they all waited at the front door as she anxiously rang the bell. What if Anne wasn't here? Why on earth hadn't she, Melanie, telephoned just in case? Her fears were soon banished as the door opened to reveal an extremely dusty looking Anne. Streaks of dirt adorned her nose and forehead, and she was dressed in an enormous sweater, that had seen better days, and patched up jeans. However, the surprise and pleasure on seeing the identity of her visitors were evident. She unselfconsciously grabbed Jake by the arm and hauled him over the doorstep followed by the others. 'Jake . . . just the muscle man I need. Mine aren't up to the job in hand . . . it's nearly toppled over me twice.' Then, remembering her manners, 'Hi, you two, nice to see you all again. Park yourselves somewhere comfortable, Jake and I won't be long.' As she disappeared into the bedroom with an amused Jake.

Chloe looked at Melanie and giggled as she raised her eyes upward in exasperation. She could hear Anne instructing Jake to 'mind the rug' and then 'a little to the left'.

'Oh no . . . ' Melanie groaned out, 'not that wardrobe.' Sure enough, as she satisfied her curiosity, there was the old clumsy wardrobe being eased, by Jake, into its new position along the wall. Jake looked none the worse for his strenuous work apart from a streak of dust on his cheek.

'Anne, did you have to move that of all things. It's too massive to lug about. What if we hadn't decided to come today? You could have done yourself an injury trying to shift that thing about.'

'Leave it, Melanie,' Jake silenced her scoldings.

Anne threw him a grateful glance and quickly wandered out to make them all some coffee.

'I think I deserve some coffee after shifting that great thing,' Jake called out at Anne's retreating figure and Melanie tried to stifle a giggle. 'What's up with you?' he queried as he dusted his hands together.

'Just a smut on your nose . . . it looks cute . . . hang on,' and she leaned on her tiptoes to wipe the offending mark away with her handkerchief. Just as she made to turn away, Jake caught and held her by the shoulders. His grin was mischievous and his eyes danced with laughter as he stared down at her face. She wasn't quite sure what would have followed had Anne not interrupted them with cries of 'Coffee up!'

They lunched at one of the city's oldest hotels, their lighthearted chatter drew frowning glances from the more staid clientele, but they took no notice whatsoever. Jake looked years younger and much more approachable in this mood as he teased Anne on her boyfriend's absence. Robert had gone to York to visit his parents for the day. Anne had not wanted to go, and had decided instead on her spring cleaning act whilst her flatmate, Susan, was also home for the weekend. After lunch, Chloe expressed a desire to see the river, and so they wandered along the river bank. The path was narrow in places and overshadowed by the trees and Anne walked ahead, holding the little girl's hand in case she slipped and fell down the steep side of the bank into the water. Melanie and Jake walked side by side behind them and suddenly, as they reached a narrower part, she felt Jake's hand encompass her own, holding it firmly but gently between his sure, capable fingers. She didn't care to look up into his face, in case he saw the tell-tale colour rising in her cheeks, but they sauntered on and he made no attempt to release her hand. Later the path took them towards the great Norman cathedral and they weaved their way up the steep, cobbled street towards the green that preceded the entrance into the massive building. Jake bent low to utter softly in her ear, 'Enjoying it, hmm?'

'Lovely, Jake.' The colouring deepened in her cheeks as he gave the hand, still in his, a gentle squeeze. Was he referring to the outing or the hand-clasp? Her fanciful thoughts decided on the latter. After the tour inside the cathedral, Anne insisted they all return to the flat for tea, and so, armed with all kinds of delectable pastries, they crammed into the tiny kitchen to prepare the meal. Jake and Melanie were banished into the sitting room and Anne and Chloe decided to take charge in the kitchen. Before Melanie realized

Jake's intention he had pulled her down on top of his body as he lounged on the sofa. The suddenness of the movement brought her close to his body; with a feeling of inevitability, she relaxed in his close embrace as his mouth caressed hers, long, deliberate and hard kisses as passion deepened between them. He kept her face close to his with his hands and, breath intermingling, their lips almost touching, he whispered, 'I love you.'

The sound of the door opening made her spring away from him just in time, although she couldn't stop the guilty colouring of her face. Jake eased himself into a more comfortable position on the lumpy sofa. She was irritated to notice that he had recovered his equilibrium perfectly at the intrusion of the other two, as they brought in the laden tea trays.

Dusk was falling by the time they left the city outskirts. Chloe was tired, so Melanie and the child were settled in the rear seats of the car. Chloe nestled against Melanie and was soon fast asleep. Nobody seemed inclined to talk very much and only then very quietly so as not to waken the child. Jake glanced in his rear mirror. 'The flat is cute . . . I can picture you living there, before.' Melanie would have liked to have answered that perhaps she would no longer be going back to live there in the future but didn't dare to presume so much, so soon. Instead she answered, 'Anne was delighted we came. She seemed quite sad when it was time for us to go . . . I'm glad you came with us today, Jake,' she ended softly, as she stared at him in the mirror.

His eyes met hers. 'So was I.'

As they turned off the main road to weave their last few miles home, Chloe stirred restlessly.

'I don't feel well, Mel'nie, my tummy jumps.' She twisted and turned to lie in a more relaxed position on the back seat. Melanie recognized a bilious attack coming on; the child's forehead was clammy and feverish and she hoped they would reach home in time.

Jake drove as fast as he dared, trying to soothe his daughter, telling her that it wouldn't be long before they reached home, and winding down the windows to give her some fresh air that seemed to help Chloe. As soon as he pulled up outside the house, he carried Chloe up the stairs and had just managed as far as the bathroom before the child was miserably vomiting. When the spasms subsided, he ministerd to her himself, refusing the assistance of the two women. Later Melanie sat up with Chloe, now sleeping peacefully in her bed, taking turns with Rose. Perhaps Jake was not such a careless father after all. She had been impressed with his concern for Chloe tonight, could she have been entirely wrong about him? And all the time, at the back of her mind, the thoughts of his declaration of love. She could hardly wait until morning to see him. Surely they would sort some kind of future for them. But it was not to be, as Melanie looked disappointedly at the note she found under her bedroom door next morning. 'Didn't have a chance to tell you last night. Will be away all week. Must meet my publishers and discuss work in London. See you at the weekend. Jake.'

★ ★ ★

The summer was giving signs of being on the wane, which wasn't very surprising in these northern regions in the middle of September. Just a hint so far, a slight drop in temperature during the day, which meant that Melanie and Chloe abandoned their sojourns on the beach; and at night, there was a distinct nip in the air and now and then, the visible signs of one's breath feathering ghostlike in the night air. Soon autumn would be upon them and she wondered if she would be here to see the russet colours appear or later the wilder, ferocious grey and white beauty of winter. For officially, her post was only a temporary job and as Chloe seemed

146

completely recovered from her convalescence, anything could happen. Nothing definite had been stated between her and Jake and indeed with his absence from home she thought her attraction was tenuous. Hadn't Rose already warned her of his amorous interludes? The thoughts that she may just be another one of his affairs did nothing for her peace of mind. On the other hand, she would not believe that his avowal had been anything but sincere.

On the Saturday that Jake was due home, Melanie took Chloe out for a drive. He wasn't expected until late evening, anyway, and to mope around the house was more than she could bear, especially under the keen eye of Rose. They decided to visit Holy Island again, a few miles up the coast. They had been to the island several times and it was Chloe's favourite spot for picnics. Especially exciting to her was the journey across the causeway linking them to the mainland, and sometimes they had crossed it safely with just minutes to spare before the tide was due to turn and the island became duly isolated.

As they returned up the drive, Melanie's heart missed several beats on noticing the Jensen parked in the drive. Behind Jake's car was Simon's white sports model.

'Daddy's back,' cried Chloe, jumping up and down in her seat. She clambered out the car and made a beeline for the house to meet her father. Melanie followed a little more sedately behind, although as excited as Chloe to greet him.

He must have just returned for she noticed he was still attired in his dark city suit and he always changed straight into casual clothes when he came home. The woman seated beside him on the sofa was breathtakingly beautiful, with her long blond hair curling around her elegant shoulders. The woman turned to appraise Melanie thoroughly, a look of cool assurance in her gaze as she took in her windswept, dishevelled appearance standing awk- wardly in the doorway of the lounge. Simon jumped to his feet to break the sudden silence. 'Well . . . the elusive Miss Crighton, at long last.' He held out his hand to her. 'Come and sit beside me and meet my sister, Sonia.'

She had to be satisfied with a cool nod from his sister as she said her 'hello's' and sat down quickly beside Simon. For some reason she was shy in meeting Jake's steady gaze as they faced each other. 'Well . . . er . . . didn't expect you to arrive so early, Jake.' Her voice almost inaudible with shyness and she dearly would have wished this first meeting to have been made when they were alone.

'Yes . . . well. I'd had enough of London and wanted to get home as quickly as possible.'

Had Melanie the courage to meet his gaze she would have interpreted the message of his eyes, but Simon noticed and frowned.

'Perhaps you knew Sonia was coming home too, Jake. Anyway, let's all celebrate the occasions tonight eh? Sonia and I shall call at seven,' Simon turned round to look at Melanie, 'so don't keep me waiting, hmm?'

'It'll be just like old times . . . eh, Jake, darling. How many years is it?' Sonia spoke for the first time since Melanie had arrived and her voice was all and more that she expected to accompany such rich good looks. She looked over to Melanie and hesitated before the deliberate words, 'I understand you're paid to look after Chloe.'

Disparaging bitch, thought Melanie violently, and threw a warm glance at Jake with his swift reply, 'Sonia, I don't know how we managed before Melanie came. She's almost one of the family now . . . isn't she pet?' Chloe nodded vigorously up at her father, sitting in the curl of his arm. Sonia wasn't too keen on the 'family' remark, Melanie noted, as she saw the girl's features sharpen in dislike at his words.

* * *

'You look gorgeous, Melanie . . . better than that horrible woman. I don't like her and told Daddy so when they went. She looks at me horribly . . . I hate her, I do.' Melanie could have heartily agreed with the child's dramatic words but wisely said nothing. She stooped to kiss her. 'Auntie Rose says that you've been allowed to sit up a little later tonight and watch the television with her. Be good, mind.'

Simon and Sonia had already arrived and Jake was busy pouring drinks in the lounge. The two men looked very attractive, but Jake had the edge in commanding her admiration with his dark, rugged looks. Sonia, as she knew she would, looked enchanting in her white pleated silk gown, her hair dressed in grecian style to complement the cut of the dress. She looked like a Greek goddess with her tall beauty.

Over drinks they chatted for a while. At least the others did, Melanie was content to sit and listen, hoping the pink dress did not compare shabbily with the other girl's creation. She had to admit Sonia could hold an interesting conversation, recounting weird and interesting tales of her touring on various assignments. She could certainly hold her audience's interest.

'Do you think you'd like a career like that, Melanie? You seem enthralled with Sonia's anecdotes.'

'Oh, but I think one has to have special qualities to manage such a job,' and at Sonia's enquiring look, 'I mean, for one thing, you would have to be able to look after yourself in tricky situations.'

'Hmm . . . well I don't think you . . . ' Jake looked squarely into Melanie's eyes, a humorous expression on his strong face, 'er . . . would fit the bill. Having had first hand experience of seeing Melanie trying to do just that . . . look after herself in a tricky situation.'

Now the other two threw puzzled

glances at Melanie and Jake, and she could have hit him at his arrogance. She well knew he was referring to the first time they had met. The night in York when he had gone to her aid because of the man in the bar. Jake drained his glass and stood up indicating it was time they left and Melanie was thankful that he didn't enlighten any of them about the York escapade.

The men decided to take two cars and Melanie climbed, resignedly, into Simon's car as Sonia was already making her way towards the front passenger seat in Jake's Jensen.

'You don't stand a chance, darling, when my little sister's around. Throw yourself on my charms instead, I'd be a willing victim.' His voice was bitter as he steered the car, following Jake out of the drive.

Melanie felt cold at his remarks. 'Are you implying that I throw myself at my employer?' Her tone as icy as she felt.

'Calm down, honey, calm down . . . you're not the first female to be

floored by Jake Masters and . . . no
. . . I did not mean that you throw
yourself at him. How do you think I
feel, you're my date, remember?'

Melanie felt terrible at their bickering
and apologized to Simon and hoped
that they would enjoy the evening in
better harmony than this. Her words
were enough for Simon and he grinned
in better humour, their sharp words
soon forgotten.

As they drew up to the hotel, Jake
and Sonia were already making their
way inside. They met in the bar for
further drinks before dining and talk
became general and lighthearted between
them all. The meal that followed was
delicious although Sonia did tend, after
a while, to monopolize all the conversation. There was dancing to a light
orchestra at the centre of the room and
during a brief lull in Sonia's, account of
her exploits in the Far East, Jake caught
and held Melanie with his eyes.

'Dance?' he inquired as he stood up
and held out his hand for Melanie to

precede him out into the dancing couples. She didn't dare to look at Sonia who she could sense was glaring furiously at her.

'Dance, little sister?' Simon was genuinely amused at Sonia's fury; he knew her only too well and felt a twinge of misgiving for Melanie.

'Oh shut up . . . and you don't seem to be charming the 'young lady' very well. What's the matter, lost your style?'

Simon's face darkened with temper at her outburst and then quickly recovered his humour for she was only venting her frustration on him and he was experienced enough to ignore her tauntings.

Meanwhile Jake had drawn Melanie well into the centre of the tiny dancing space. The place was crammed and one could do no more than hold one's partner closely and shuffle around the floor. He pulled her into his arms in the anonymity of the couples surrounding them, and his hands, underneath her long hair, caressed her naked back.

He groaned softly as he buried his face in her hair near her ear, his body as close to hers as possible. 'I've been waiting to do this to you all day, kitten.'

In answer her hands crept from his shoulders to the back of his neck to caress his hair at the nape and he strained her closer still to him until she breathlessly told him she was unable to breathe. The lights had dimmed at the next dance number, a slow, dreamy love-song and Jake held her still on the floor, not wanting to turn back to their table just yet. His nearness and the haunting quality of the song were enough to make her quite happy to remain where she was. At one time in the semi-darkness he lightly rested his mouth upon hers, and the contact, his nearness and the clean, male smell of him set Melanie trembling with arousal that was unbearable in this so public yet almost private surroundings.

'Don't . . . ' she murmured, turning her head away from his and she felt his whole body stiffen at her withdrawal.

Almost immediately he pulled away from her, and she could see his eyes were glittering with anger. The dance had not yet ended but without a further word said between them, he had guided her off the dance floor and back to the table. Melanie's first feelings were of despair; he had misinterpreted her action and she wanted to quickly explain but the cold scowl on his face turned her thoughts in likewise anger at him. Suddenly unbidden thoughts of what the housekeeper had said to her came into her mind, perhaps he just didn't like being thwarted from his own pleasures. Where women were concerned, he controlled them like putty in his hands, malleable for his own desires. The more she looked at his sullen expression, the more she was convinced that was the reason for it.

Sonia's eyes wore a malevolent expression as they approached the table which quickly turned to frowning puzzlement at the faces of Melanie and Jake.

'Darling Melanie, you needn't sit yourself down.' as Simon got up to stand near her, he put his hand on her wrist and she was surprised to feel his clasp was a strong grip that brooked no refusal as he led her back onto the dance floor.

'Phew . . . thank God for that. I couldn't have stood another minute of it,' Simon muttered in her ear as he drew her into his arms, not as tightly held as Jake would have done.

'What on earth do you mean? As she drew back to look up at him, Simon gave a derisive smile and drew back to rest his face against her hair. She noticed dispassionately that no leaping response came from her own body in answer to his.

'My dear . . . I've warned you about my darling little sister before. Although she wouldn't dare give Jake the lashing of her tongue. Still, she did stay with him at his London flat this week.'

Melanie's blood froze at his idle words. Stayed at his flat — this week whilst Jake was away — they were there *Together*. Oh God, what a mess she had got herself in. And there he was playing up to her on the dance floor, a few minutes ago . . . on and on ran her erratic thoughts. If only she could retrace the last few minutes, how differently she would have behaved to him when he held her in his arms, murmuring sweet nothings in her ear. She gave a bitter smile at her reflections.

'Is that true?' she asked of Simon in a low voice.

'Sure . . . look honey, their particular affair has been going on and off for years.'

Melanie felt a particular kind of distaste at questioning Simon at this moment but she had to know the truth. 'Well . . . how long do you mean? . . . I mean . . . that is . . . their . . . affair.'

Luckily Simon was only too willing to tell Melanie the story.; it would be advantageous to him, he knew, to get Jake Masters off the horizon where

Melanie was concerned and continued to tell her, in a low voice so as not to be overheard by other dancers surrounding them on the packed floor. 'Well actually, it started about ten years ago, when she was only nineteen. Oh, don't get me wrong ... she knew her way around in the big wide world, even then. Come to think of it she was a precocious kid sister as long as I could remember, from a very early age.'

Melanie did a bit of mental arithmetic. 'Well, why didn't he marry her instead of Marion?'

Simon raised his eyebrows at this question. 'You know about Marion?' At her nod he continued, 'We have been doing our little homework, haven't we?' But at the warning expression of her dismayed face he apologized for his remark. 'I'm sorry, honey, I don't blame you, in a way.'

After a few minutes he answered her question, 'I don't think Jake was ever the marrying kind. When we were at university, I noticed Jake was never short of girlfriends.' A wistful note crept into his voice, and she wondered if Simon was envious of Jake. Surely not, he was a handsome man and she reckoned he also would have left a trail of devastated hearts in his student days. 'Why Jake actually married, I'll never know. Perhaps she told him she was pregnant . . . I don't know. Sonia, I would have said is made from the same mould as Jake . . . the non-marrying type. Lately, 'tempus fugit' as one would say, well, she's not getting any younger. I feel a change in their relationship, I think she wants Jake permanently, and in an official capacity, as her husband.'

Melanie pondered on these words; there could be an element of truth in them. But Jake was already married and she spoke of this to Simon, 'So what?' he answered. 'There's divorce . . . don't worry, Sonia won't let that interfere with her plans.'

Melanie gazed into a sea of anonymous faces dancing around them and then Jake and Sonia came into her line of vision, dancing closely. Her scarlet fingernails gleamed in the subdued lighting as they clung to his neck, like some feline predator. And then Melanie, dismissed her sour thoughts, despising her jealousy. She couldn't resist another furtive look as they shuffled around the floor; Jake didn't seem to mind Sonia's lover-like hold, and, unable to bear the sight any longer, asked Simon to take her back to their table.

'Sure, honey. Another drink would be a good idea. It's thirsty work, dancing all night.' Melanie couldn't resist giggling at him as they left the floor, and Jake watched their every movement as Sonia snuggled even closer to him amongst the throng of dancers.

As the evening advanced, Jake noticeably drank more heavily, Melanie was amazed that it seemed to have no affect on him whatsoever, but nonetheless it didn't stop her worrying about what possible state he could end up in. Simon and Sonia showed no concern about him. Indeed, Sonia was acting like the cat with all the cream, Melanie miserably noticed. She hoped her own bright fixed smile looked natural enough to the others, when inside she could have sobbed in her anguish. Jake said very little in the way of conversation, but then Sonia was quite happy to monopolize the table, holding their attention about her brilliant career and exotic travels.

What a disastrous evening Melanie thought, as she began to eye the rest of her party with sudden distaste. Perhaps she, too, had drunk too much for her depression was beginning to overwhelm her with her oppressive thoughts. She felt a little guilty for Simon; if he only knew her thoughts as he gave her an affectionate glance as Sonia droned on. She knew it was her own dismal spirits which were colouring her attitude at the little party. She was beginning to wish it was time for their departure home and was surprised when Jake started to break up the proceedings by saying it was time they were headed for home. No one raised any objections to this and they gathered outside in the car park, Melanie hugging her woollen shawl tightly round her in the chilly, night air. To everyone's surprise Jake indicated for Melanie to get in his car and she could tell Sonia didn't like it at all.

'Well what about coming back to our place for coffee?' she said protestingly. Jake had already got in the car and refused for both of them. Melanie was glad he had for she had no desire to continue the evening's entertainment. Sonia stormed off — after very brief goodnights were said — into Simon's car as Jake reversed out to drive onto the main road. Melanie gave a warm wave in goodnight to Simon as they passed by. He rolled the window down and shouted something at her but Jake was driving past and she couldn't hear his words.

The return journey was made in silence until they had pulled up in the drive of his house.

'Well? Had a good night?' His words were almost mocking but she ignored the taunt.

'Yes thank you.' She could sense he was spoiling for an argument and refused to be drawn.

'Good.'

Jake opened the front door to allow her through and said he would put the car into the garage. She left the door open for him and hastily made for her room. She wanted no more encounters with Jake for a while, verbal or otherwise.

6

There was no sign of Jake the next morning as Melanie hurried down, a little late in rising, for breakfast. She had lain awake a long time, unable to stop thinking of his affair with Sonia. The answer was in her own hands; ignore his attractions and get on with the job that she was here for, forget what had transpired between them. So engrossed in her problems it was a few minutes before she noticed that Rose didn't seem in too good a mood either this morning.

'Something wrong, Rose?' she asked as she observed the thin, tight smile as Melanie greeted her.

'You might tell me,' was the enigmatic reply, then she was suddenly absorbed in frying the bacon and eggs with unusual care and attention. Chloe wandered through, causing the subject to be dropped. But after the meal, the child asked if she may watch Mason, the gardener, reorganize the greenhouses this morning and so, as soon as they were alone again, Melanie pursued the matter.

Rose wore a worried look on her face as she exhaled her cigarette smoke. 'Well he's not his usual self at all, this morning . . . and that's a fact.'

'Oh.'

'Something's on his mind . . . bothering him. I've never seen him polish off a bottle of scotch as a nightcap for a long time.'

'Oh . . . you've seen him then . . . today?'

'Of course,' Rose answered irritably, 'I always take him an early morning cuppa in bed.'

'What happened then?'

'Well first of all, he wouldn't have the curtains open as I went to do just that. Then when I slid a closer look at him . . . I thought he might be ill, you know. Anyway, there was this empty whisky bottle by the bed. He went to sleep, I think, so I went downstairs and checked the liquor tray and sure enough, he'd drunk the lot.'

'He seemed alright last night when we came home.' Although Melanie couldn't quite meet the older woman's gaze. Well he did, didn't he?

'Are you sure, Melanie?' The house-keeper kept her gaze on the girl, waiting for her answer.

'Yes . . . yes, of course . . . unless . . . Sonia upset his cool.'

'Hmm, I doubt it, he's used to her type,' Rose musttered as she got to her feet to clear away the dishes.

★ ★ ★

'Hello, hello, how are my favourite girls today?'

Melanie looked up from the absorbing task of mowing the lawn. Simon's tall, debonair frame was a welcome sight strolling across the garden. Nobody had encountered Jake all day and the tension was building up in Melanie to such an extent that the strenuous activity of gardening had seemed a good idea. She straightened from the backbreaking task as he tugged, playfully, at a strand of Chloe's hair, who had been following Melanie with a rake to tidy the new cut grass. She wished that she didn't feel so hot, and surely her face was damp and flushed with her exertions, it certainly felt it. To Simon, she looked delightful, her face free of cosmetics, glowing; indeed, he couldn't resist the urge to plant a quick kiss on her nose.

'You never kissed me,' said a small plaintive voice.

'Then I shall soon remedy that, my sweet,' and Simon picked up a squealing Chloe and swung her around, high in the air, before he planted a resounding kiss on her cheek. Simon's cavalier actions brought grins from them both as he proceeded to roll Chloe about on the newly mowed lawn. Melanie, too, got caught in the spontaneous horseplay, trying to extricate Chloe, a giggling, helpless Chloe, from his clutches only to find herself on the grass with a laughing Simon holding her down by her shoulders demanding submission.

The laughter quickly died as she surveyed the unsmiling features of Jake above Simon's left shoulder from her restricted worm's eye view. Her distraction was quickly conveyed to Simon, who, on looking round and seeing the reason for her sudden, guarded expression, slowly released her. Suddenly Melanie felt foolish and guilty at the fun they had just shared.

'I hope you haven't been too rough with Chloe, Simon.'

'Of course not. Chloe's not an invalid now, Jake.' The injustice of Jake's remark had prompted an immediate response from Melanie in Simon's defence. But the bleak look on Jake's face caused her to say no more as he stared directly at her with a look almost of hatred. Simon summed up the situation at a glance and, taking Melanie by the shoulders, he suggested they help themselves to a cool drink indoors.

'Methinks I could cut the atmosphere with a knife where you and Jake are concerned, my sweet,' Simon whispered in her ear as he led her towards the house, followed by Jake and his daughter.

As they sipped their drinks, Melanie glanced surreptitiously at Jake as he talked to Simon. He didn't look as if he'd been 'hitting the bottle' the night before. Although she recollected that he had drunk quite a lot at the hotel, previous to that, and it hadn't affected his equilibrium then. Chloe drained her glass noisily and, wiping her mouth, announced that she was going back to continue her gardening chores. Simon also finished his drink. 'I think I'll join you Chloe. Come on Melanie, let's take advantage of the warm sunshine . . . it is rather cool in here.' He set down his empty glass and followed the child out of the room. Melanie made a move-ment to follow him but Jake forestalled her at the doorway and, before she realized his intention, and had closed the door; leaning against it, he faced her, standing only inches away from her.

Melanie's heart leapt at the quickness of his action and, as she tried to back away, his hand lashed out and caught her arm in a hard, decisive grasp. His grey eyes glittered like icicles and her throat went dry as sandpaper as she stared back at him apprehensively, her eyes wide with fear.

'What the hell do you think you're playing at?' The question was almost ground out at her. Jake's face was tight with anger or maybe some other emotion, Melanie couldn't be sure. Could it be jealousy?

'I beg your pardon?' she questioned haughtily, trying not to let his nearness reduce her to trembling awareness.

'You blow hot one moment and cold the next, when I'm around.' The grip he had maintained on the upper part of her arm relaxed for an instant only to draw her nearer to his body, 'don't start behaving like a bitch Melanie, it's not in your make-up.'

She could feel the warmth of his breath on her face and the panic started to well up inside her as her traitorous body responded sensually as she came into contact with his hard, muscular chest.

Anger with herself for weakening at her resolve if only for a moment to keep out of any further entanglement with Jake caused her to struggle fiercely against his grasp. 'Let me go, they'll be wondering where I've got to . . . please Jake.'

'They . . . they . . . ' Jake bit back an epithet. 'You mean Simon will be wondering . . . don't you?'

Never before had she seen Jake in such an icy temper and she gazed in wonderment that she had caused this mood in him. There was no doubting that he thought she was playing up to Simon's charm. Well, wasn't that all to her own good? Didn't she want this to happen? The contempt he held for her was there in his eyes as he stared angrily back at her. Wasn't it what he only deserved? He, too, had had no scruples about his own amorous affairs. The arguments whirled round in her head and exploded in bitter retaliation at his next words.

'Lover boy a better prospect than me, is that it?'

She wrenched herself out of his fingers at last and almost spat the words back at him. 'At least he hasn't got a wife to run behind when things get too hot for him.'

As soon as she had said the hateful words her mind was horror-struck at the vindictiveness of her statement. How could she accuse him unjustly, for there was not a shadow of doubt in her mind that he would never ever need to use his wife's name in this way. She would have wished for anything not to have said those detestable words to him.

'You bitch!' he exclaimed in a low

passionate voice as he dealt her a resounding blow with the flat of his hand on the side of her face.

Just as Melanie was horrified at her angry words so was Jake at his own savagery. Disgust with himself and concern for Melanie wiped away all that had passed between them in the last few moments. His blow had been all that she had deserved in Melanie's estimation of herself, but for all that she couldn't stem the flow of self-pitying tears that welled up in her eyes and started slowly to tumble down her cheeks. Typically as only women can be, she couldn't bear to allow Jake to see her in her distress and turned away wanting only to get away from him and up to the privacy of her own bedroom before she broke down entirely and sobbed her heart out in front of him.

'Melanie, oh, Melanie.' Jake's voice was full of contrition and he tried to gather her in his arms to wipe out the hurt he had inflicted as if she were a young child. 'Oh God, what are you driving me to do? I've never touched a woman like that in my whole life . . . please believe me, darling, I'm sorry, don't cry so.' His voice was full of concern and self disgust at himself, as he continued to murmur against the side of her face that was now red with the marks of his hand The feather-light kisses he tenderly gave her as he stroked her hair, her face now hidden in the hollow of his shoulder, were anything but childlike. Slowly, as he continued to placate her, Melanie's hushed sobs subsided and she became conscious of his trembling body pressed against her own and the sound of Jake's hoarse murmurings as his mouth trailed fire down the side of her face and neck.

The sound of Simon's voice in the hall brought them both back to startling reality as they sprang guiltily apart. Melanie panicked at the thought of Simon finding her in such a state as she hastily tried to scrub the evidence of tears that had ravaged her face. Jake looked at her for one moment, his face registering understanding, and, placing a finger gently to her mouth to be silent, he opened the door to meet Simon.

'Do you know where Melanie's got to Jake?'

'Er, I believe she went upstairs to freshen up first, she probably won't be long.'

'Oh good. By the way, come and have a look at the mower, I don't know what I've done to it but the damn thing's gone on the blink.' The sound of Simon's voice trailing away as he obviously was moving back to go out of the garden filled Melanie with relief as she leaned for support against the other side of the door. She thought Jake must have hesitated and then muttered an assent at Simon's request for a few seconds later, he, too, could be heard walking out of the hall. Waiting a few moments longer and hoping Mrs Kennedy wouldn't be around any-where, she hesitantly opened the door and seeing the way clear made a beeline for the safety of her own room.

It was a good half hour before Melanie had the courage to return back into the garden and face them all, most of all Jake. She had washed and applied a light makeup to conceal the ravages of her tears but still had to lie down on her bed for a few minutes to calm her trembling emotions. The most strongest feeling was that of her shame for the bitter words she had hurled at Jake and she knew that no matter what happened after, she would never forgive herself for launching that particular form of verbal attack at him.

As she walked out onto the lawn where Jake seemed to be still tinkering on with the intricacies of the lawn mower only Simon looked around at the sound of her footsteps, and holding out both hands at her, remarked on how long it took a female to freshen up. She mumbled out an apology about a sudden headache probably brought on through her earlier activities under the hot sun. Simon was immediately contrite and insisted she sat on one of the loungers, anxiously drawing one of the umbrellas near to her for shade, for all she tried to convince him it had now cleared. Jake merely looked around at her as he still crouched over the troublesome machine; his glance told her nothing except perhaps polite interest. She sighed inwardly to herself, and as Simon, too, drew up another lounger beside her for himself, she decided Jake's manner was for the best and tried her hardest to interest herself in Simon's chatter and forget the turmoil of the last hour.

After a few minutes it wasn't very hard to laugh at a few of Simon's witticisms, for he could be very entertaining at times, all part of the charm he could practice so effortlessly. However, no matter how hard he cajoled or pleaded, he couldn't pin Melanie down to a definite arrangement for them to go out for an evening in the near future. Jake could hear every word of exchange between them but his expression never changed from that of his absorption in the mower. Simon invited himself to tea and shortly after departed for home, not before learning that Jake would be returning to London the following week; that bit of news was very welcome to him indeed and assured Melanie and Chloe that he would be a frequent visitor in the coming days to relieve their boredom. Jake's dry comment that they had managed quite comfortably to amuse themselves without, Simon's presence went by unnoticed except by Melanie, who, sitting nearest to Jake, heard the muttered aside. She wasn't sure whether she, too, was pleased, relieved or just plain disappointed at Jake's departure tomorrow.

Later, in the early evening, she took herself off for a walk along the beach. Chloe was being supervised by the housekeeper and put to bed earlier than usual as she had looked very tired after the pleasure of their toil, and the child had not complained at the housekeeper's suggestion for an early night.

The picnickers had deserted the

beach, leaving evidence around of their recent feasts Melanie looked about her with distaste at the clutter of papers and cartons. Shrugging her shoulders at the debris she strolled along the sand, walking near the shoreline, where the ground although damp was easier to walk along than slithering on the fine deep sand near the dunes. As her gaze fixed on a slither of driftwood gently rising and dipping on the slow moving waves, but relentlessly being brought in on the incoming tide, she thought how symbolic of her own present state. No matter how hard she decided on a course of action planned to ease her situation, like the feeble piece of driftwood, so were her emotions caught up in a stronger current out of her control, the outcome of which she was unable to decide. Her determined resolve of this morning to place the relationship with Jake on a more impersonal footing had crumbled in the few seconds it had taken for Jake to stop her at the lounge door. She knew that she had no defences against his attraction and that his power over her gave her no peace of mind.

As she let herself into the house Jake appeared from the lounge doorway.

'Melanie.' He raked a hand through his hair as he studied her with an anxious look in his eyes. 'I wondered where you had got yourself to. I tried your room and when you weren't there I thought maybe you had taken Simon up on his offer of a date.'

She stood uncertainly in the hallway and couldn't make up her mind whether to join him in the lounge or go upstairs. 'No, I just went for a walk along the beach.' Deciding to be a little more prudent and go to her room she proceeded to walk slowly past him towards the stairs.

'Melanie?'

She turned hesitantly, 'Yes?'

'Care to take a stroll down the village with me, er, for a drink.' He grinned suddenly at her and that was enough to banish her sombre mood as he went on, 'no strings . . . just a drink. I could do with a change of scenery tonight.' For a fleeting second she wondered if he was going to visit Sonia tonight and had decided he had had enough of the Armstrongs for a while and then dismissed the thought as wishful thinking on her part.

'Okay, give me a couple of minutes.' Melanie raced up the stairs and deciding not to change her denim jeans or shirt as she reached her room. She glanced in her mirror and pulling the bunches that were now all tangled with the sea air, released them from the bands and brushed her hair quickly, leaving it loose about her. A quick application of lipstick was all she dared allot herself and, not wanting to waste any further time, she joined Jake downstairs, waiting in the hall for her.

He, too, she noticed with relief, was dressed very casually: in black cords and sweater giving him a sinister appearance with the scar adding the final touches, and the thought caused her to smile unwittingly.

'What's the joke?' murmured the voice above her head as Jake ushered her out the door.

When she explained to him at first he didn't grin in amusement but commented that his satanic looking scar was enough to frighten anybody off.

'Oh, but I didn't mean . . . ' she faltered, her heart dropping like a stone at her heedless gaffe, anxious only to make amends, 'What I mean is . . . I don't think it's ugly.' His sudden grin stopped her from saying anything further and they proceeded to walk slowly, side by side, although Melanie was careful not to come into contact with his hand nearest her own, on their way to the village.

The small bar was practically empty and Jake told her to take a seat while he ordered the drinks. As she sat by the window, he was greeted by the land-lord, who obviously knew him, and after a few desultory remarks about the late summer weather, Jake strolled over to her with their drinks.

Ignoring the seat opposite, which she thought he would take, Jake sat down on the small window seat beside her, seemingly completely at his ease although Melanie felt herself tense at his nearness. At first nothing was said between them and Jake calmly sipped his beer as she tried to relax by studying the interior of the pub.

'I've never been in here before. It's quite cosy, isn't it?'

'Hmmm.'

Gradually the tension eased out of her and after several sips of her martini, she began to relax beside him.

'That's better, you were like a cat on hot bricks when we first came in here.' That comment from him caused her to giggle and suddenly the tension did indeed disappear and they chatted about anything inconsequential and she took the opportunity to gaze at him without causing unnecessary interest from him in return.

For Melanie, the time flew on wings, and with a start she heard the landlord asking patrons to finish their drinks.

'Goodness, Jake, it must be getting late. I didn't realize the time.'

Jake finished his drink and rose from his seat. Smiling at Melanie, he extended a hand to her to assist her out of the window seat.

'C'mon, then, let's weave our way homeward.'

They shouted their goodnights to the landlord. The pub had filled up considerably since they had first come in and he returned their farewells, shouting likewise against the din of his regulars. The night was all around them as they walked in the direction of the coast road, there was no wind, the air was still and quiet as only a summer's night can be, and as they walked down the deserted road, Melanie shivered slightly for the thin shirt wasn't very warm at this time. She felt the warmth of Jake's arm as he gathered her close to him in the night air.

'Cold?' was his only remark.

Melanie didn't or couldn't reply to his remark. His nearness, once again, had affected her and the tension suddenly built up around them. Slowly they walked closely down the lane, the man's arm protectively draped around her shoulders, their bodies in close contact with their movements until Jake came to a slow stop underneath the branches of a weeping willow cascading over an old stone wall on Melanie's side of the road.

She couldn't read the expression in his face for there was no street lighting around them but he drew her round to face him, both his hands strong and firm on her shoulders.

'I truly beg your forgiveness for my brutal action this afternoon, Melanie.' After a short pause he continued in a low voice, 'I absolutely hate myself for it.'

'Oh no.' Melanie's heart melted at the agony in his words. 'No, Jake, I was just as bad, please let's forget it altogether.'

After a short silence, in which Melanie held her breath in awaiting his reply: 'I don't think either of us will forget it, forgiving will do.' His words were slowly said almost as if he were uncertain in some way.

'I forgive you then Jake.' She felt a shudder of relief pass through his body and at his near inaudible murmur of 'Pax?', so too, did it seem the most natural thing for him to lower his head and rest his mouth against her own trembling lips, as she too whispered the same word in reply.

The echoing footsteps of other people walking towards them along the lane broke the tender moment. Perhaps it was just as well for she would have flung her arms about him in wild response, wanting only to cling to his tall frame and lose herself in the passion that could have followed as his mouth began to harden against her own soft mouth. Jake idly swung her hand in his as they resumed their walk on homewards and Melanie refused to think of the day they had shared at Durham when he had declared that he loved her, that would be confusing her thoughts too much.

The delicious aroma of an itinerant van advertising the sale of fish and chips made Melanie realize she was starving, or perhaps it was merely the appetising smell that made her wrinkle her nose in appreciation.

'Want some?' Melanie couldn't believe she had heard right but when Jake repeated his question and declared he was famished, her enthusiastic nod was enough in reply.

'C'mon then,' he said as he hauled her off in the direction of the well illuminated van. Never had Melanie enjoyed a meal so much. As they munched their way along the road and Jake crumpled the discarded newspapers in his hands and left them in a convenient litter bin she heard him comment, 'It's many a year since I indulged myself like that.'

'Then you should indulge yourself more often,' came her tart reply.

Jake stopped in his tracks and chuckled menacingly at her. 'I know what I'd like to indulge in . . . come here, woman.'

'Not on your life . . . lecher,' she threw back at him as, still giggling, she ran the last remaining yards down the drive to the house. Jake started an immediate pursuit and they were both brought to an abrupt halt, Jake almost colliding into the back of Melanie at the figure about to get in her car parked outside the doorway.

'Oh, hello, Sonia.' Melanie wished she didn't look so dishevelled or that Sonia could look so beautiful, it didn't help her morale too much.

Sonia chose to ignore her greeting and her narrowed gaze rested on Jake and then widened in disbelief at the horseplay that they had both been enjoying and brought to such a sudden end.

Jake was the first to break the frozen silence, 'Sonia . . . is anything the matter? I thought you were going back to London today.'

Sonia's smile was wide and confident, as somehow brushing past Melanie she linked Jake's arm as he walked with her back to her car.

'That's just it Jake, darling. I decided to return tomorrow instead and when Simon told me you, too, were going, well . . . I thought we may as well travel down together. I do so hate long journeys on my own. Now what time are you coming to pick me up?'

'Well . . . I'm not sure myself . . . ' but Sonia would not be put off at his hesitant words. 'Look, come over and pick me up about ten. I'll be ready and waiting.' Sonia was climbing into her car and, after a brief wave at them both, drove off leaving Jake and Melanie standing looking on at the retreating car.

Suddenly the night had lost its magic for Melanie and, mumbling a goodnight to Jake she mounted the steps into the hall. Her action seemed to provoke Jake out of his reverie and shouting, 'No . . . wait . . . ' he also joined her in the hallway.

'Before you go to bed, there's something else I want to talk to you about.'

'Okay, what?'

'It's about Simon Armstrong,' and he could feel her stiffen as he held her arm.

'Yes?'

'Let's have some coffee, hmm?' Not waiting for her consent he opened the kitchen door for her to precede him.

Sighing, she entered the kitchen and busied herself arranging cups as he discovered a thermos of coffee, already prepared by Rose and thoughtfully left for their use. She was half way through her coffee and still Jake had not spoken as they sat at the kitchen table.

'Well, what about Simon, Jake?'

Draining his cup, he rose and moved round to her side. 'I've got to know before I go away tomorrow . . . does

Simon mean any more to you than as an . . . old friend of mine?'

She hesitated, wanting to find the right words yet unable to understand the urgency of his question. 'He's a good friend. I've enjoyed his company . . . nothing more than that.'

'That's fine then.'

'I'll say goodnight then Jake. Oh . . . have a pleasant journey tomorrow.' Melanie was already moving towards the door as she spoke to him, unable to bear the tension that had sprung between them.

'Goodnight, Melanie.' Jake remained in the kitchen as she hurried upstairs. If only he would ask me what he means to me, her heart cried out, if only he would tell me what I mean to him. That's all that matters.

★ ★ ★

The week dragged slowly by and the following Wednesday, Simon phoned to invite her and Chloe over for the day, to which Melanie readily agreed. The delight in Simon's voice was unmistakable. 'Great. Expect me in about half an hour,' and he hung up.

Simon's parents were charming and considerate, like their son, and they placed Melanie completely at her ease. She hoped Simon had not given them the wrong idea about their, Simon and Melanie's, relationship; his proprietary manner as he placed an arm along her shoulders and propelled her slightly forward as he introduced her to them gave her an uneasy suspicion that he may have just done such a thing.

'And this is Melanie.' That was all he said in actual words, but the tone of his voice belied the simplicity of his statement. Melanie's anger was brief and momentary for she had enough troubles without imagining even worse complications. For all that, it was a most enjoyable day. Chloe, like any other child, was utterly fascinated by the tour of the farm. Simon gave her a ride on one of the small ponies in the paddock which she enjoyed immensely. There were no opportunities for Melanie to speak to Simon alone, for she would have liked to question him about Sonia's departure to London. Had Jake picked her up to journey together? She knew jealousy nagged, like a toothache, but Sonia was so beautiful, Jake was no saint, she knew only too well.

Simon brought them home about five and Melanie was about to get out of the car to follow Chloe, who was already racing up the hall steps when he put a restraining hand on her arm. 'What about dinner . . . tonight?' He pleaded with her and she found his actions grating on her nerves.

'No . . . no . . . no I don't really think . . . ' she began irritably, unable to give a reasonable excuse.

'Alright.' This time there was no mistaking the hurt in his voice.

'Later in the week, perhaps,' she relented, ashamed of herself.

'Friday then . . . I'll pick you up at seven. Okay?'

'Okay.'

Simon took her up the coast to a small country pub, nothing as pretentious as the elaborate hotel of his previous dates. Something was wrong with him, she had tried several times to make idle conversation but Simon seemed preoccupied.

'How long do you intend to work for Jake?'

The suddenness of the question caused her to merely stare at him and then ask the reason why he should want to know.

'I wondered if you thought it a long term arrangement,' was his oblique answer.

'No. Of course not.' She took another sip of her vodka and speaking more slowly as if she weren't really answering Simon but thinking out aloud her thoughts. 'Come to think of it, Chloe is almost recovered now. Really Jake should have sent her to school. I'm not sure about his future plans concerning her, Simon.'

'Then you would expect to be leaving in the near future anyway.' It was some moments before the last word he uttered registered in her mind and then a feeling that something unpleasant was about to unfold caused her hand to tremble, spilling a little of the spirit in her glass. 'Anyway?' she repeated at him.

'Come on, let's go for a drive . . . the air's a bit stuffy in here now.' Simon rose and held out a hand to usher her out of the room. There still weren't many people in the small lounge, but they could have conducted a private conversation without being overheard. She was impatient with him at not answering her back. Presently, as she knew he would, he drew the car along a deserted part of the road and, pulling off a little way to the side, he cut the engine. Melanie looked at him in the gloom and waited expectantly for him to speak.

'I want you to be my wife.'

Melanie's jaw sagged open in utter astonishment at his proposal and

Simon, now looking directly at her, noticed the mixture of emotions so apparent on her face as he switched on the interior light of the car. Surprise quickly ebbed, followed by dismay and the anger on his face was exposed to her in the dim light.

'Simon, I . . . I . . . ' she stammered, not wanting to hurt him, but he caught her arms in a harsh grip. 'It's Jake, it's been him all the time, hasn't it?' came his taut rejoinder. Angrily he threw her to one side. 'You're an utter fool, Melanie. Jake outgrew girls like you when we were at university together.'

'I don't want to hear any more. Take me back home.' She covered her ears, like a child not wanting to hear something bad. She felt a glimmer of truth in what Simon was trying to say to her. Well the truth hurt and the look on his face told her there were more hurts to come.

'Melanie . . . Melanie . . . ' He slowly gathered her back in his arms and his gentleness was balm to her bruised feelings. 'I know you don't love me . . . but if you married me . . . it would work . . . I know.'

She stiffened but he pressed her head back against his chest and slowly stroked her hair soothingly. 'You know I adore you . . . it must have been pretty obvious, the way I've been hanging round Jake's house since I came home.' He cupped her face between his fingers and the love was there for her to see as he looked deeply into her eyes. 'We could make a good marriage. It's time I settled down and the parents think you're a 'grand lass'. Please say 'yes' darling . . . please.'

She allowed him to kiss her mouth for his hypnotic words had produced a dreamlike quality around them. Wouldn't it be better to take what Simon had to offer? The sincerity of his words were without question and he was a very attractive man, no financial worries either. Melanie chided her thoughts at the mercenary ideas and inwardly despised herself for even thinking along those lines. Perhaps he sensed her withdrawal for his kiss became more passionate, almost desperate and his hands were no longer gentle but hard with the urgency of his desire for her to succumb to his demands.

'Please, no . . . stop it . . . Simon . . . ' She struggled within his embrace and at first he paid no heed whatsoever, allowing his frustrations to take over. She became still and the action forced Simon to realize his lost cause. They drew apart, and he mumbled a quick apology which Melanie brushed aside with a shake of the head. Reaching for his cigarette case, he allowed a breathing space of time to recover their normal calm.

'Cigarette?' he offered. She shook her head and after he lit his own said, in a dull, flat voice, 'Sonia rang me today.'

'Oh . . . is she having a good time?' Her voice, edged with sarcasm.

His laugh was bitter. 'I never heard her more happy in my life. Jake's been to see his wife. He wants a divorce.'

'What . . . How does she know this?' She hardly recognized her own strangled voice.

'Darling . . . if Sonia says he's getting a divorce, then that's the truth. If you had heard her on the phone . . . crowing about imminent wedding plans. Probably Jake told her . . . after all she's staying at his flat . . . so . . . ' He shrugged, completing the misery his words had given her. 'What about us?'

'Us?' she queried.

'Does it give me any more hope . . . that perhaps you've changed your mind?'

'Oh, Simon.' She slowly shook her head, her shoulders sagging with dejection. Without another word spoken, he started the car and reversed out onto the road.

7

By the end of the second week of Jake's absence, even Rose was a little bewildered at having received no word from him. She had gone to the extremes, as she later told Melanie, of ringing his London flat and a man called Williams, his manservant, had informed her that Mr Masters had been called away on urgent business. Jake had apparently given him strict instructions not to reveal to anyone, no matter what the circumstances, his forwarding address. He did know where to contact him in emergencies but as Rose Kennedy certainly couldn't give such a reason, she merely thanked Williams and rung off. As she told Melanie the news it was obvious to the girl that the housekeeper was extremely worried. If she knew, really knew, that Jake was beginning to tire of his latest amour in this case she suspected Melanie Rose didn't dare consider the consequences. For hadn't she grown to be very fond and attached to Melanie and her worst possible fears were to be realized? God forbid.

The following Monday they received a visit from Sonia. It was hard to gauge who was the more surprised, for different reasons: Sonia, on learning that Jake was not at home and Melanie, that Sonia had indeed come home.

'Well I rang the flat and Williams told me Jake had left.' Sonia's haughty attitude as she wandered about the lounge grated on Melanie's already taut nerves. At least Williams musn't have given her any information either, Melanie noted with satisfaction. She enquired politely if Sonia would like some coffee and at her imperious nod, scurried out to the kitchen.

Sonia was graciously draped against the sofa when she returned with the tray. Her airforce blue suede outfit was a perfect foil for her long blond hair, casually styled today, swept away from her face and highlighting the perfect bone structure and clear skin of her face. As they sat opposite each other sipping their coffee, Melanie couldn't think of a single thing in the way of social chit chat. Surely those lovely dark eyelashes weren't real? Melanie wondered as she stared at Sonia, preoccupied with lighting a cigarette. Resignedly she had to admit they were indeed natural and Sonia caught her intent gaze and matched it with one of her own. Serves me right, thought Melanie glumly, as her cheeks burned with embarrassment.

Trying to retrieve command of the situation, Melanie asked various idle questions on her recent trip to London. For once Sonia was not inclined to elaborate, answering Melanie's polite questions with barely worded replies. Eventually, she gave up trying to rouse some sort of response from Sonia and sat, drinking her coffee in silence and wondering why Sonia didn't make a hasty exit as Jake was the person she had come to see, not Melanie. She looked up and this time caught Sonia staring at her, a thoughtful expression on her face.

'Tell me,' Sonia said as she exhaled her cigarette smoke, 'have you got another job lined up when your er . . . services are no longer required here?'

Bitch, thought Melanie, but instead said in a saccharin voice, 'Mr Masters hasn't dismissed me yet.'

'Well you know what I mean . . . It could never have been a permanent arrangement, now, could it?'

Conceding defeat, Melanie shrugged, sick of the interrogation. 'It won't be very difficult for me to get another job.'

'What have you been doing to my brother while I've been away?' And, as Melanie looked puzzled, 'He's a bit down in the dumps these days, talking about cutting his leave short and going back abroad to work.'

After Melanie's non-committal reply, Sonia launched her attack. 'Isn't he as good a prospect as Jake? Perhaps that's the trouble.' Noticing the easy flush on Melanie's cheeks and then the sudden paleness, she misunderstood her reaction.

'You're wasting your time,' Sonia's features were distorted in her anger, 'a nobody like you. In any case Jake and I have had an,' she hesitated, 'an arrangement for some time.' She continued to smoke her cigarette, a little calmer at the look of dejection in Melanie's transparent emotions passing across her face, clouding the bright look in her green eyes.

Well, she didn't have to sit here and listen to that cat gloating over her triumph, and with this decision in mind, she rose suddenly. 'Excuse me please, you don't have to spell things out to me.' She turned in the doorway and, glancing back at the still-reclining figure, added: 'Mind you . . . took you some time . . . didn't it?'

Melanie had no compunctions whatsoever in her parting shot, in fact she had derived a small amount of satisfaction from delivering it. Sonia certainly deserved the jibe.

That night Simon phoned Melanie, the first time she had talked with him since the night of his proposal. Her heart had raced at the sound of the telephone bell as she was coming down the stairs and the nearest to answer it. Her first thoughts were of Jake, it must be Jake, after all this time.

'Melanie?'

He must have heard the disappointed tone of her voice through the receiver. 'Oh, Simon . . . yes?'

'I wondered if I could see you tonight, perhaps a drive.'

Melanie started to refuse but he interrupted her quickly, 'Look, I'm going back overseas tomorrow. This is my last night in England and I would very much like to say goodbye to you in the flesh . . . not some disembodied voice over a phone.' After a few seconds' silence he added, 'You could at least give me that, Melanie.'

'Of course, of course, I was just wondering about Chloe ... er, what time?' She lied convincingly for he told her he would be along in half an hour and hung up, presumably in case she changed her mind, for he didn't even wait to say goodbye or check if the time was okay by her.

Sighing, she replaced the receiver only to find the housekeeper hovering in the background an anxious expression on her face. 'Er, was that Jake, Melanie?' Shaking her head in answer she mounted the stairs to her room and explained as she made her way up the steps that she would be going out and didn't expect to be long.

Simon took her to the local pub, the same one that Jake had taken her to that other memorable night. The landlord greeted her as they entered the small bar, although he didn't seem to recognize Simon, but greeted him politely, just the same. She didn't know what to say to Simon; what was there to say to him? He didn't act the rejected suitor type, but was just as debonair as ever, elegantly dressed as usual, his handsome face smiling and carefree as she would always remember him. Why couldn't she have fallen for him instead of Jake? Simon must be the easiest person to live with his general *joie de vivre* attitude, his attractiveness, were no mean attributes. Instead the image of a dark, satanic face, scarred and sensual, a man of many moods, some of them unpleasant, focussed in front of her, and she felt an actual physical pain at the thought of what could have been . . .

'Hey . . . don't go into a trance!' Simon snapped his fingers mockingly in front of Melanie's dreamy eyes.

'Wha-at . . . oh, sorry.' She brought her mind back to the present and gave her companion a beaming smile.

'That's better, now drink up, I want to celebrate tonight.' He threw her a wicked look. 'Escaping from the matrimonial hook for one thing.'

They had a good evening together;

another good point in Simon's favour was that he held no emotional grudges and, as the evening wore on and several drinks had flowed by their way, he began to expand more on his 'lucky escape'. She decided that his talk wasn't just sour grapes for, as he reasoned, with the life that he liked to experience — such as travelling abroad, working on desolate sites that were no place for a woman to be anyway — a marriage would have certainly hampered his career. There was plenty of time yet for him to get married and maybe have a family, but his keen interest in his work commanded that he not retire to some desk job as yet.

'Mind you . . . we would have made a beautiful relationship, darling.' His blue eyes deepened at the prospect. The invitation in his eyes was like lighting a fuse to the already sensitive feelings of his partner, especially after the intoxicating liquor that Melanie had consumed, and Simon's arm moved closely around her shoulder at the unexpected response.

As they came out of the pub a few minutes later, Melanie still felt in a slightly bemused state and the fresh air did nothing to revive her. Weakly, she clung to Simon's arm as he guided them round the back of the pub to his parked car. The gravel path she walked along felt like a small hill, the ground sloping alarmingly.

'Oh dear . . . Simon, I feel very . . . giddy.'

'Never mind love, cling on to me.' His voice was soothing, sympathetic.

He drew his car up at the front of the house and gently shook her awake, feeling slightly apprehensive, for he blamed himself for her tipsy state. 'Melanie,' then more urgently, 'Melanie . . . please, we're here . . . for God's sake . . . '

'Mmmm?' was her only response.

Slowly her fuddled brain returned to consciousness and she looked over to the anxious-looking face of Simon gradually clearing as he observed her returning to near normality.

'Simon,' she whispered.

He cupped her face between his hands. 'I hope you find your happiness, my love. And I wish you all the very best, you deserve it.'

Simon kissed her slowly, his mouth warm and caressing. She couldn't stop herself remembering the feel of another warm and compelling mouth that could turn her blood to molten lava. Perhaps this thought connected itself in the strong response of her own mouth, and she kissed Simon as fervently back. This reaction affected Simon strongly, his arms coming around her shoulders, down her back as he tried to gather her closer to his body, the pressure on his mouth increasing. Eventually, she realized her silly action and gently brought the embrace to an end.

'Goodnight, Simon. Thanks for the evening.' Melanie quickly clambered out of his car, her head still swimming with the sudden action as she stood and waved him off up the drive. Slowly she entered the door, still unlocked and mentally thankful that she hadn't to fumble in her bag for the key.

Oh dear . . . She clutched the side of the wall as she manoeuvred her body along the hall to the foot of the stairs.

'Melanie,' the voice boomed and echoed to die away in the distance and suddenly there was Jake by her side, and a very angry look on his face. Why did he always seem to look at her angrily? and she must be dreaming to see him here now.

'I'm dreaming, aren't I?'

'And I thought he didn't mean anything to you . . . a good friend, no more, some friend.'

'Oh for crying out loud, shut up . . . ' Even in her state she surprised herself at her brave words and said in a softer voice, 'Please Jake, not now. I feel awful and . . . ' Horror followed her stumbling apology as she felt unpleasant sensations going on around the region of her stomach 'Oh no . . . I think I'm going to be sick.'

Without another word spoken between them, gently Jake ushered her up the stairs and along to the nearest bathroom. Weakly she protested that she would manage on her own, but he would not leave her until she had reached the comparative safety of the cool, tiled room, and thankfully for Melanie, he left her, still without saying a word, merely shutting the door behind him.

Afterwards she felt better, leaning against the cold tiles for a few minutes, absolutely disgusted with herself at getting into such a state. She sluiced cold water over her face and gingerly opened the door. No sign of Jake; perhaps it had been her imagination after all. The door to her room seemed a long way to walk but slowly she groped her way along. Never had she celebrated an evening and ended up as bad as this before. A weak smile formed on her mouth as she reminded her brain to write about the event in her next letter to Anne. She'd get a telling off in return, no doubt about that.

At first she didn't notice the figure standing by her window as she closed the bedroom door behind her, leaning against it thankfully at not encountering the housekeeper or Jake.

'Oh no . . . not another lecture, please,' she murmured as he slowly walked up to her still leaning against the door.

'It's okay, don't worry . . . come on.' His voice was low and soothing, as if he were talking to Chloe.

It eventually dawned on Melanie that he meant to undress her and put her to bed and she protested feebly as he firmly drew her coat from her shoulders.

'You needn't go all shy and modest; tonight, at this moment, I'm thinking of you as I do of my daughter . . . lift your arms.'

Eventually he drew the bedclothes over her now nightdress-clothed body and she marvelled that she wasn't embarrassed at his actions.

'See you in the morning,' he murmered as he straightened and looked down at the nearly sleeping form, shaking his head in exasperation at her. The next time she opened her eyes, Jake had disappeared out of the door.

The next morning she gingerly eased her body out of bed, careful not to make any sudden movement in her fragile state. She was surprised to find no symptoms of any shattering headache and as she slowly got her bearings walking round the room to collect her toilet bag and dressing gown in preparation of her way to the bathroom, she didn't feel so bad after all. There were no signs of any hustle or bustle down the stairs and no tantalizing aroma of frying bacon either; frowning in puzzlement she walked along the corridor to her shower.

Peeping in the lounge on her descent from upstairs she found Jake lounging on the sofa watching television, although she amended that discovery to the fact that the set played to a deaf audience as he seemed more interested in the sheaf of papers scattered around him, spilling onto the nearby coffee table.

He sensed her silent entry for he suddenly looked up and raised his eyebrows as if she were an apparition standing there, hovering at the door.

'Good afternoon, feeling, er . . . alright?'

'Afternoon?' she answered back, a horrible feeling settling in her stomach.

'Er . . . it's about,' Jake looked at his gold wristwatch encircling his wrist, 'ten minutes past two,' and looked back at her with a slow grin appearing on his rugged features, altering his scarred face to a more gentle expression. He could see that Melanie felt a little uncomfortable at her apparent laziness and tried to put her at her ease.

'Don't worry . . . you're not quite in everybody's black books. Mrs Kennedy decided to have a day's shopping in the town and Chloe wanted to go with her, so . . . ' He shrugged as if that completed his answer, as Melanie muttered that she would make herself some 'breakfast'.

Oh dear, what a thing for her to do . . . not only disgrace herself with her most unladylike manner of the night before . . . She blushed at the thought of Jake undressing her for bed; she hadn't made much of a fuss at the time but without the alcohol in her bloodstream to dull her wits . . . no, she'd try and put that out of her mind.

'Want any help?'

She spun round at the unexpected question, wishing Jake would go back into the lounge and resume whatever he was doing, as she busied her hands with opening the cupboard doors in the kitchen.

'Okay, okay, I'll make myself scarce . . . but do you feel alright now?'

'Yes thanks.' Surprised and pleased at his concern.

'Good, I knew a good long sleep would do the trick,' and he paused before disappearing back out of the door, wicked amusement gleaming in his eyes, 'and when I peeped in at you this morning, all tucked up fast asleep

. . . I gave strict orders to the other women in this house to leave you alone.' Noticing her flush and satisfied that he had succeeded in confusing her once again. 'Oh, and I didn't elaborate to anyone that you were busy . . . sleeping it off,' with great emphasis on the phrase. 'Mrs Kennedy didn't know what time you came home last night so I hinted that Simon had taken you down to Newcastle to celebrate and so it was the early hours of the morning before you returned.'

'Oh Jake,' Melanie protested, making him return at the raised tone of her voice, 'what will she think I am, did you have to say that to her?'

'The lesser of two evils, my sweet,' and he disappeared before she could make further protest.

Muttering to herself, she prepared her coffee and, not sure about the state of her digestive system, she decided to settle for a couple of slices of toast as her breakfast-cum-lunch meal. She wondered how long the older woman would be away. Probably until the late afternoon, she knew that Rose Kennedy liked a whole day devoted to her 'looking round the shops', and hoped that Chloe would behave herself during the outing.

After she had finished her little 'snack' she knew she would have to join Jake in the lounge; there was nothing else to do. A light drizzle had formed outside so an excuse of going out for a walk would have seemed very peculiar indeed, and to retreat back to the solitude of her room would more than likely encourage Jake to come and seek her out in case he thought she was still 'feeling a little poorly'.

She seated herself on the sofa opposite Jake and picked up a discarded newspaper to amuse herself with for the next few minutes. He glanced up from his papers and smiled absently at her. As if he had forgotten her existence he continued to read in apparent concentration. Gradually she relaxed in the quietness, a cosy atmosphere pervading the room. They could have been an old married couple, sitting in the lounge, idling the afternoon away. No . . . put those ideas out of your mind you silly nitwit, she silently berated her fanciful mind, and concentrated on the latest world events of the day.

She finally succeeded in losing herself in her newspaper, for she started at the sudden movement of Jake as he got up, tidied his papers in a neat stack and, placing them on a side table near the door, returned to sit near her on her own sofa. She could feel the nearness of his hard thigh close to her own as he draped an arm negligently along the back and settled into a more relaxed position. She knew he was facing her although she had tried hard to keep her face fixed on the paper on her knee, her head bent in apparent interest in the print.

'Let's talk.' Jake's voice was soft and inviting, putting Melanie straight on her guard; now what did he want?

'What about?' She looked at him and drew back immediately at the nearness of his face only a small distance away.

'Oh . . . anything, I feel the need of your company . . . and you can be quite amusing sometimes. Tell me what's happened while I've been away.'

'Mrs Kennedy was quite worried about your disappearance act,' and she caught her breath in the slip she had just made, Jake was very perceptive.

'She rang the flat.' His voice sharpened in question. 'She's never said anything, did something happen that I should have been told about urgently?'

'Oh no, no . . . ', she fumbled about for the explanation to have tried to contact him at all and decided the truth was the only answer, 'you had been away longer than your usual times . . . Mrs Kennedy was anxious and contacted your man, Williams.' She finished her excuse lamely, hoping he would leave things at that, and breathed a sigh of relief as he shrugged as if dismissing the subject, yet hoping that she would indeed find out why Jake had disappeared for a while.

'Sonia called yesterday.' She watched his unresponsive expression with interest: not the action of a man intending to marry Sonia and as he did not take up her statement, she prattled on, albeit a trifle nervously. 'She was very upset that you weren't here.'

Still Jake never bothered to remark on the subject and feeling a little bolder she pursued the subject. 'She'd rung your flat, you see.' At this Jake stirred himself enough to make an answer, a little interested at last perhaps in Melanie's chatter.

'When?' And then, 'I suppose when she was staying in London.'

'Oh no,' Melanie interposed, 'no, I believe when she came home.' Her suspicions were well and truly roused; thoughts jingled about in her mind, as she tried to remember what Simon had said, surely he mentioned that Sonia was staying at Jake's flat? Yes, she was certain he had said just a thing. Now how could she have done that after Jake insinuated that she couldn't have been staying there? It didn't sound as if he hadn't been telling the truth, when he naturally assumed Sonia had rang him when in London herself. Therefore, Melanie logically concluded, Jake and Sonia must not have contacted each other whilst both in the city — or only rarely perhaps.

So absorbed in her conclusions was she that she didn't, at first, notice that Jake was slowly moving nearer until she felt his warm breath on the side of her face. A large masculine hand crept round her shoulder and gently reached up to command that she turn to face him. She felt herself holding in her breath in anticipation of . . . she knew not what . . . but Jake's mouth was smilingly tender as he looked down into her eyes.

He could feel the trembling that the touch of his hand on her skin had provoked, that could trigger off his own response to her nearness.

'Oh . . . Melanie,' he started to say in a slow voice, deep with meaning, 'let's put all the differences we've had together in the past and start again, hmm?' The seductive quality in his voice made her a willing, acquiescent victim to his demands as he tentatively parted her lips with his mouth; lightly at first and, as her breathing quickened, with more pressure, that caused the heat to flare between them from their mouths and coursing through their bodies.

'Oh no, don't,' she breathed against his face as he continued to place his mouth gently around the outline of her own mouth, 'I can't think straight, please . . .'

'Don't think, darling, just enjoy what we've got between us . . .' He raised his head a fraction to look straight into her eyes. 'Something great, isn't it?' he whispered and on a low moan lowered his mouth to seek the passion within her own.

She couldn't think, only sink in the

sensual vortex of their close embraces and let herself drown in the pleasures that Jake's love-making were arousing. With gentle pressure his body, hard with the tension of his own feelings, pushed her back, until they both lay side by side along the sofa. Her brain just barely conscious of his hoarse passionate murmurings, she moaned with the intensity of sensation that his hands stirred as they caressed the soft flesh that he encountered as his fingers urgently pulled her blouse from the confines of her waistband.

Revelling in the intimacies that they were delightfully sharing, she traced his scar with her mouth, the tip of her tongue lightly tracing its path from his brow down to his eyebrow, and the action surprised him and caused a momentary delay in his kisses as he looked at her, with eyes aglow with desire for her, and resumed his exploration of her throat. 'Oh God, how I love you . . . it's been agony away from you, darling . . . wanting you, thinking of you all the time,

the sleepless nights you've caused me
. . . all I want out of life is you.' On
and on he muttered, like a man in
torment as his passion increased, thrill-
ing Melanie to the core of her being
with his words and loving. 'Just let me
love you . . . and love me back.'

In slow reaction his words registering
in her brain reminded her of his recent
absence from home and, like an acid in
her mind, the thought of a divorce being
mentioned by Simon, concerning Jake,
leapt in her forethoughts. Of course, it
was for her, Jake wanted to marry her
. . . not Sonia, and then, her confidence
failing, and the acid doing its deadly
corrosive work — could it be for Sonia
— and was Jake using her for his own
selfish pleasures.

The very dread that these thoughts
imparted caused a stillness in her
previously responsive body, at first
unnoticed by Jake, and then he
gradually withdrew to look down on her
face, unable to understand the cooling
of her ardour.

'Jake?' she moistened her suddenly dry lips 'What am I to you?'

He couldn't understand her nervousness either. 'I've told you . . . I love you, isn't that enough for a woman?'

'No, Jake . . . it's not enough at all. Not for me, anyway.'

'I see,' in a quiet voice that filled Melanie with an unnamed dread.

'You want it signed, sealed and delivered first, like all women.' His lips twisted cynically and his eyes clouded with hurt. 'I've yet to hear you love me, for that matter.'

'You know I do,' she answered quickly.

'Then you know how wonderful our life can be together.' He took the opportunity to gather her back into his arms. 'These feelings we can bring out in each other, the loving we can give; oh God, Melanie, what else matters in this world?'

'You happen to have a wife somewhere, Jake. Are we supposed to forget her?'

This time Jake stiffened at the

mention of Marion, and he closed his eyes momentarily. He knew this would happen, been almost prepared for it, yet still, when he was faced with such an insurmountable problem, the thought of losing Melanie now . . . well, it couldn't bear thinking about. Long ago, he had scorned the solemnity of the marriage, Marion had seen to that, but he could understand this innocent in his arms; yes, he could understand her fears.

'Is it true that you've approached her about a divorce?' Her question was startling to his ears.

'Where the hell did you hear that from?' She could detect a desperate note in his question.

'Is it true, Jake?' she repeated.

'Yes, damn you.'

'And what about Sonia?' Her heart dropped at the anger in his answer and she waited, like a condemned prisoner, for the death blow.

'Sonia?' His look was incredulous. 'Sonia . . . what are you getting at?

What's Sonia got to do with our bloody affairs?' Anger exploding within him, his face white at her probing.

She sighed with relief. She had certainly been told a whole pack of lies concerning Sonia, and quickly related to Jake what she had heard from Simon. He patiently allowed her to finish her rush of words, his face darkening against the thoughts of meddlesome Simon.

'Sonia has never stayed at my flat . . . ever . . . and Sonia means nothing to me, nothing. The divorce was because of you.'

'Oh Jake, that's marvellous, oh, darling, I'm sorry to have behaved like that.' She completely overlooked the dullness of his answer or the grim look to his mouth.

'There's going to be no divorce, Melanie. I don't want to say any more on it.'

The silence was shattering. She looked in disbelief at his face, but the set features answered without the need for any words.

'But why?' She shook her head unable to envisage a life without him. 'It's not because of religion.' He shook his head and she took a deep breath and continued in a shaky voice, 'You can divorce her, Jake. I'm not very conversant with divorce procedure, but . . . we can supply the evidence, can't we. I wouldn't mind the publicity if it were worth it for us to start a new life together.'

'I wouldn't ask you to do such a thing, even if it were possible. No, Melanie,' he turned to look at her steadily, 'there's to be no divorce, ever. I can't explain why to you, just trust me.'

There was nothing more said between them for a few minutes that felt like an eternity for both of them.

'We can't go on like this.' She protested in a strangled voice.

'I don't expect us to.'

'I'll have to leave here, Jake.'

'No, don't do that . . . I couldn't let you leave me, not now, darling.' He grasped her cold hands in his own, pressing his mouth to them in a despairing manner.

Realization of what he intended grew in her mind and she felt old and sad at the thought. She couldn't understand why there could be no divorce, she was sure he didn't need his wife's permission after all these years. Surely he had enough grounds now, desertion? . . . he hadn't led the life of a celibate since their separation, and she shuddered at the word, adultery.

'Has the ring got to be on your finger?' He suddenly got up and paced the floor knowing deep down inside him that he was fighting a losing battle. 'Melanie . . . this is the nineteen-seventies, people aren't going to lose any sleep at the fact we won't be married. It's what we have between us that matters. Why . . . even Chloe, young that she is, would grow to understand in time.'

'You're asking me to live with you.'

'Why not? It's all I can offer . . . yet I will love you all my life.'

232

'No, Jake . . . I can't do it.'

'Trust me just trust me, Melanie. Don't walk out of my life. I plead with you to stay.'

She couldn't look at him, not wanting to see the matching agony of his own gaze and, unable to bear it any longer, stood up too, determined to end this painful scene.

'It's no good, Jake. That kind of life is not what I want or believe in. There's nothing further to say to each other.' She quickly reached the doorway. 'Without acting like a melodramatic heroine . . . you realize that I will want to leave now, this minute. It won't take me long to pack . . . ! Bye Jake.'

She was frozen of any feeling whatsoever as she raced up the stairs to pack her belongings, no tears would fall until perhaps this numbness would wear off. Mechanically she groped for her cases and like a robot started to go through the cupboards. The sound of her door slamming shut told her that Jake was standing there and she turned slowly to face him. His face was pale with the agony of his dilemma, he couldn't let this woman out of his life, and his eyes registered his desperation.

He was at her side in two strides and clutched her by the shoulders, his hands like steel vices that gripped so strongly, and she winced at the bruises that would appear.

'Perhaps if I took your love you'd stay, you have no idea what kind of living you're sentencing me to, with your decision to go.' His mouth was hard on her closed lips, determined to wield his power over her. She struggled against him until he forced her against the side of her bed and they sank on it, the weight of his body over her own, pressing her down into the mattress. She fought his caresses madly until eventually, as she feared, she could no longer prevent her own desire for him, and as before, her hands had caught at his hair to pull him from her. She tangled her fingers through the ruffled locks and stroked the back of his neck.

She couldn't resist the feelings that ignited between them and arched her body to his and gave herself up to the passionate demands, not protesting as he feverishly undid the buttons of her blouse, but moaned at the sweetness of his touch on her breasts. Jake was no longer in command of himself, he had wanted her too long to try and stop his love-making. She caressed the dark hair on his chest as he quickly undid his shirt and then his mouth clung to hers, claiming his need of her.

'Love me, Jake . . . love me.' Her arms caressed the smooth skin of his back, the muscles rippling under her fingers, trembling with her need of him.

'Mel'nie . . . Mel'nie . . . are you up yet . . . where are you? Daddy . . . Daddy.'

They lay on the bed, motionless, becoming alive to the surroundings and very much aware of the child's voice in the hall downstairs, childishly shouting for them; only their intermingled heartbeats, racing erratically at what had passed between them, each knowing that Chloe's arrival had stopped an irrevocable situation.

A shudder of defeat went through Jake's body and, sighing, he released his weight over Melanie and slowly got off the bed. Running his fingers through his ruffled hair and then buttoning his shirt and tucking it back in his trousers, he looked down at the still figure on the bed. He knew it was over, the dead look in her eyes, eyes that had been aflame with want of him only seconds or heartbeats ago.

'I'm still going, Jake. Regardless of this.' Her hand motioned the bed and their recent passion.

His scar was white against the darkness of his face, and suddenly he looked older, the weariness of his lost fight showing in the dejected figure as he faced her across the bed. Disgust with himself, his pride in ashes at the seduction he had intended, would leave a very bitter taste in his mouth. And like a wounded animal he lashed the words back at her.

'Then go, damn you, go.' He turned back once as he made his way to the door, his lips curling almost in hate at the girl, still lying on the bed. 'I wish I'd never set eyes on you, my life was at least bearable. Take your virgin little body and scuttle back to Durham, get married, make it all legal. I thought you were different, but you're just the same, deep down, as the women I've met up with in the past. No . . . you're worse than them. At least I enjoyed my moments with them. You . . . you've been nothing but trouble. You've taught me my lesson, I'll give you that consolation.'

Thankfully he had gone when the harsh tears spilled onto her cheeks, they had shared enough misery together, enough to last a lifetime.

8

The evening still held a promise of warmth after the heat of the day; in these northern climes, it wasn't expected to enjoy a heatwave in early June. Most people had taken advantage of the lucky weather. Melanie's place along the river where she usually sat, eating her lunch, was taken by a group of youngsters. Bearing no grudge against them, she walked further along the bank and sprawled on the grass, near the water's edge. She was unaware of the appreciative glances from the young men passing by, a small, slim figure with her hair neatly coiled on the crown of her head. As she chewed her sandwiches, she debated whether to call on Anne and Robert this evening. She knew that they always made her very welcome in their new semi-detached that Robert had purchased just before the wedding six months ago.

Remembering Anne's wedding stirred painful memories that she found unable to forget. Looming up in her mind was the image of a tall, scarred man stern and forbidding, deep and passionate, warm and tender . . . she remembered all his moods so well. For during the hectic plans when arranging her friend's nuptials, it had been a blessed relief at the time to be immersed in something to occupy her thoughts some of the time to be and that interim period had erased some of the hurt she had suffered on that last, disastrous day at Cliffe House. She had kept her word to Jake and left within the hour. Luckily, she saw neither Rose nor Chloe, for she could not have disguised the ravages of tears or the deep unhappiness in her eyes. Jake, too, had not been around anywhere, although she thought she glimpsed his tall figure looking out of his bedroom window as she drove out of the drive, out of his life.

Eventually, after a few weeks of moping about the flat, a vacancy had turned up at her old office. She had exhausted the generous cheque that Jake had forwarded on to her — and she had suffered no qualms in cashing it, he could afford to be generous, couldn't he? Anyway, she reasoned, it was salary due to her. She noticed bitterly that he had not bothered to write an accompanying note with the money. Services rendered . . . Now when she thought of him, only a deep hurt remained. She knew she loved him just as strongly, for her there could be no one else. Sometimes she wondered, and worried, what was he doing now? Was he happy? She desperately hoped that he was happy, for once her hurt numbness had worn off a little, her only considerations were for him. A few weeks after her return to Durham she had read in some newspaper that he was returning to the States with his daughter. The thought then had flashed through her mind that she could have accompanied them and if she thought honestly, she admitted that had she not upheld her rigid moral principles on that fateful afternoon, she might be to be with him now. Chloe had later returned to attend boarding school in Southern England. The child had written to Melanie, having obtained her address from Rose, she had informed her friend. At Chloe's request, Melanie had written regularly, taking a great interest in her studies and asking Chloe all about her schoolwork, her teachers, the new girlfriends she had made.

After work, Melanie gave Anne a lift home. Robert was off on another work course to further his career, and promised faithfully to call round later that evening. She let herself into the flat, the same that the girls had shared before, only this time Melanie had decided she could afford to have it all to herself. Susan, admitting that a life away from her parents didn't appeal to her, had graciously left them shortly after Melanie had returned.

She made herself scrambled eggs on toast and settled down on the old sofa with cigarette and coffee. After a little while, she stirred to get herself changed and washed ready for her visit to her friend, in a small, new housing estate on the other side of the old city.

'Hullo, love, have you already eaten or shall I make you something now?'

Melanie shook her head at the seemingly unconcerned look on Anne's face at the innocent question, grinning absently at the tactics employed to encourage her eating habits. She knew she had lost a lot of weight and had become fashionably slimmer, although Anne considered she had overdone the fasting. Indeed she knew her loss of appetite in the past months had resulted in her thinness and her clothes hanging slackly about her figure. Anne always took the opportunity to try and 'feed her up' and at the same time not make too much of a fuss about the matter.

Switching off the percolator in the kitchen Anne carried through to the lounge a tray bearing two steaming cups of the delicious-smelling coffee. It took a few minutes for Melanie to realize that Anne wasn't behaving in quite her usual manner. Her whole bearing had an expectant tense attitude, and she didn't seem to be prattling on about the day's events in the office —a practice she had loved to indulge in when they were flatmates.

'Something not gone right today?' Her question was studiedly casual.

'No . . . the usual little panics at work with that new supervisor but otherwise a normal day.'

'Alright,' Melanie sighed as she offered her friend a cigarette, and after lighting them up, 'tell me what's on your mind.'

Anne seemed to be having an inner conflict judging by the expressions passing over her face, and it was some minutes before she uttered a word.

'Have you read the daily newspaper yet?' Seeing her friend shake her head she got up purposely and, bending over the magazine rack, took out the morning paper. Melanie was agog to know what was going on but patiently waited whilst Anne scanned the pages and, finding the item, folded the newspaper into place and silently handed the news over to her.

'Poor woman,' she murmured after she had read the item. Her words were an understatement in the circumstances considering she was talking about the person who had ruined her chances of a future with Jake.

'Melanie . . . is that all you can say . . . don't you realize what this means?' Anne had been told the whole sorry story by Melanie, although she had omitted the details of Jake's final physical persuasion for her to stay. Those memories still seared her dreams and gave her many sleepless nights, her body wanting him desperately, aching for his touch and the ultimate possession. How many times had she wished that he had taken her completely; she would be with him now, loving him and being

244

loved in return. That was all that matters, all that was important; at least they would have known some happiness together.

'Melanie,' Anne almost cried the word, 'he's free now.'

So Marion, Jake's wife, was dead. She wondered if Jake had known about her condition and felt compassion for the woman that had so affected her life, for all they had never met. To have died of cancer was a horrible fate for anyone, and the newspaper report had elaborated on the suddenness of the news. Apparently Marion had announced a long holiday abroad some months earlier and her stay had been instead in a nursing home on the South coast, for her illness had been a closely guarded secret.

'Will you contact him now?'

'No'. Melanie shook her head emphatically, it would make no difference. Too long a time had passed, too many angry words said between them. 'I think he hated me, I have no doubt now that I was just another woman, one of his affairs, you know.'

'How can you know that . . . you've been eating your heart out for the man all these months. I see no reason why he hasn't done the same,' Anne argued back.

'Oh Anne . . . grow up . . . love isn't all sweetness and light.' She was weary of the arguments. She had let him down, he had asked her to trust him and surely one couldn't love and not trust. But she had, she did love him, but at the time, she had thought too much of what other people had told her of his various affairs in the past. Oh, it was no good making excuses, it was her own fault.

Anyway, as the months passed, she read several items about him in the States. His name was once linked with a famous actress, there had been a picture of her clinging to his arm as they attended a Hollywood premiere. Just as ruggedly handsome but the report had caught the hardness of him, his cynical eyes blazing into the camera. She steeled herself into not keeping the picture of him and had thrown the magazine away, half unread.

Another course came up at work, and much to the astonishment of her friends and to the delight of Anne, she applied and was successful. It was held at Edinburgh and Melanie found the work interesting and applied herself to it with great zest. Her colleagues were forever jibing her on staying in the hotel every evening, working on her notes and on the last night, she relented and joined the girls on a last pub crawl of the city.

It was unbelievable how it happened: one moment she was walking along the pavement in one of the city's busy thoroughfares on their way to a lovely little pub the others had discovered, and the next moment there was Jake, only feet away, and they both spotted each other instantaneously. Carol, one of her colleagues, was walking on the outside, nearest the kerb. It had been

raining throughout the day and several
puddles lingered in the roadside; a
passing car had splattered her legs and
the party had momentarily stopped to
assist the girl in wiping the streaky
marks from her legs.

Jake was driving slowly at the time,
maybe he wasn't sure where he was
going. Melanie was standing a little to
one side of the girls as they clustered
around the unfortunate Carol woefully
bemoaning the state of her appearance.
It had been easy to spot Melanie out of
the group as they caught his momentary attention from the road.

She stood transfixed as he drew the
Jensen to an abrupt halt, leaning over to
open the nearside door and waiting for
her to get in. Typical of Jake, arrogant
enough to ignore that she may be going
somewhere important and to drop
everything and simply climb in beside
him.

'Gosh, we're in luck tonight, girls,'
she heard one of the party murmur in
an astonished whisper.

'Get in,' commanded Jake impatiently as she stared at him, feasting her eyes on the object of her dreams for the past few months. She turned to one of the girls to mutter her excuses and as Jake urgently repeated his order she mumbled a 'sorry' and quickly got in the car, leaving her friends gaping open-mouthed at their exit.

'Well, really, she's a dark horse . . . c'mon girls.' The party wandered on to their night's entertainment.

This time Jake drove faster until they pulled up at one of the more impressive looking hotels in the city. He ushered her out of the car, tossing the keys to one of the hotel staff, waiting at the door, to drive round the corner and subsequently park. Melanie was still in a daze and allowed him to hold her arm and guide her through the foyer, into a lift and along one of the corridors to his room. She guessed it must be to his room, where else could he take her along the anonymous doorways of the long hall?

Surprised at her outward coolness although inwardly her emotions seethed in turmoil of what might be said between them. For the moment it was bliss just to see him again after all this time. As he unlocked the door and stood aside for her to enter she perceived that he too was not unaffected by their sudden meeting. His face was as tanned as ever, due to his recent stay abroad she surmised, looking as attractive as she remembered him in a dark blue suede jacket with black trousers and black turtle-neck sweater.

The room was not his bedroom but, glancing at two adjoining doors off the room, a small sitting room. Of course, the affluent could always afford the best, a hotel suite nonetheless. She revelled in the unaccustomed luxury, sinking into one of the black leather armchairs clustered around a low glass-topped coffee table. Jake slung off his jacket and carelessly draped it over a sideboard that supported a considerable array of drinks for anyone's taste.

'Well . . . ' Jake hesitated, surely not at a loss for words, 'want a drink?' He turned to pour out a generous whisky for himself but Melanie declined. She felt intoxicated enough just being here with him in the privacy of his suite. Gulping down his drink he poured out a second measure and casually walked over to stand just above her.

'Won't you sit down as well, Jake . . . you make me feel nervous, towering over me like that.' Even her voice was cool and unshaking and she marvelled at her composure.

Taking her completely by surprise he draped himself over the arm of the chair in which she was sitting, extending an arm along the back of her seat, almost touching the top of her head. Melanie felt her throat drying up at this action and clasped her hands in front of her to stop their trembling.

'Wha-at, er, brought you to these parts . . . business?' This time she couldn't keep the stammer from her words.

'You might say that . . . personal business, actually.' He finished his drink and, placing the empty glass on the table stood in front of her and coolly grasped her hands in his and pulled her from the chair to stand close in front of him.

'You brought me here.' He finished quietly, staring into her eyes and Melanie felt her pulse leap with excitement at the response in his.

'Me!' she almost shouted and opening her mouth to make further enquiries was very efficiently silenced by the firm mouth of Jake as it covered her own with great expertise.

The kiss went on for light years, neither in any hurry to finish the embrace, both of them filled with such a hunger for each other as they tightened their hold. Eventually, perhaps they both realized that there were too many things to say to one another, a lot to explain, Jake gently brought the kiss to an end and as his mouth drew away, Melanie felt incredibly shy, for no reason at all and buried her head against the dark wool of his sweater, against his hard chest. She could feel the uneven tenor of his breathing as she rubbed her face against him.

'Oh Jake. I've missed you so . . . wanted you . . . ' her muffled voice whispered against his warmth.

'Darling, not as much as the agony I've been through . . . thinking of you . . . and only remembering the last time . . . that afternoon.' His hands trembled as he stroked her hair. Slowly and gently he forced her to look at him and was surprised to find tears in her eyes but a warm, shaky smile on her lips. Kissing away the moisture on her face as his fingers held the sides of her head: 'Now let's get one thing straight first and foremost.' He took the opportunity of kissing the tip of her nose as she blinked away the rest of her tears. 'I want you to marry me . . . I love you . . . and let's make it as soon as possible.' noticing her raised eyebrows he quickly added: 'Our marriage, of course.'

Trust Jake not to ask her . . . just a simple statement of fact, but her heart warmed at the prospect and she hugged him back in response, unable to speak for the joy spreading through her veins, evident in the sparkle in her green eyes and the warm flush glowing in her cheeks. She grinned back at him cheekily but in a sober tone said, 'Yes. I want to marry you . . . I love you . . . and let's make it quicker than possible.' She had hardly finished saying the words before he drew her tightly to his body and kissed her thoroughly.

'No . . . wait, Jake . . . ' She squirmed in his strong arms and, drawing back at last, her words coming out in quick gasps, 'How . . . how did you know where I was?'

'Well, I think it's best for both of us, if I start at the very beginning first, don't you think, hmm?' His hands slid down to clasp her hands. 'Get me another drink — you may as well start getting used to your wifely duties,' he said as he sank into the nearest armchair.

After handing him the glass, she knelt beside him on the goatskin rug, leaning against his knees, looking up content to gaze at the man, who, after all, would be sharing the rest of their lives together.

'You do realize why I couldn't divorce Marion now . . . I knew she didn't have a chance when the doctors told me of her cancer.' His face showed pity. 'I had been to see her about a divorce, she was uninterested and looked so ill. When I suggested she have a check up, she just laughed. I think now she was worried sick, she probably had a good idea that she had something terribly wrong with her.'

'Poor Marion,' Melanie murmured. Is everything over between you and Sonia?'

'You've given me the impression

before of suspecting something between us, am I right?'

Melanie started to shake her head but he insisted that she tell him. Sighing she told him of her suspicions and the fact that Sonia and Simon had provoked her into believing them.

'Look darling, I'll be completely honest, I have had an affair with her in the past . . . but that was years ago. We met in New York, I was staying at the same hotel. Look, honey, Sonia takes her pleasures when she wants and she never gives a damn about people's opinions. I had no illusions about her, nor she about me. I wasn't a particularly nice person in those days to know,' he added wryly.

'I know . . . Rose warned me off, she was only thinking of my own good, I'm sure.'

'I'm sure she was . . . wait till I see her again,' he added in a warning voice and, seeing the worried look in Melanie's wide clear eyes, 'Okay, I suppose she had good reason at the time.' He stroked her cheek tenderly, 'I was crazy about you, even then, although I wasn't pleased about a cheeky little brat like you being able to wrap me around your little finger.'

'Oh, Jake,' was all she could answer.

He began to lower his head and remembered he hadn't finished his explanation, shook his head, 'Anyway, the thing was, no divorce . . . I was hopping mad and pretty desperate . . . I think I knew then I couldn't have you any other way. Still, the next thing that happened was a call from some doctor in this nursing home. She had collapsed and been rushed to the nearest hospital. Of course, after their diagnosis, and the fact that she had given my name as next of kin . . . they contacted me as she was being transferred to this nursing home.'

Melanie protested that he need not go on, she had realized after reading about his wife's death that maybe he had known about her disease and wouldn't under any circumstances file for divorce.

'Well that's about it . . . she was

terrified of publicity, terrified I would say something ... I promised her faithfully and so she cooked up the idea of telling the press about her long holiday abroad.'

'You could have told me Jake,' she remonstrated quietly, and he looked long and hard at her before he answered, 'Yes, I know ... but would you have believed me ... once you accused me of hiding behind my wife when ... things got a bit hot for me ... remember.'

'Oh Jake, after all this time, just through misunderstandings on both our parts, we've gone through all this misery.'

'It was hell at first, and then I felt resigned after that ... I'd led a hell of a life before you came into my orbit ... I thought you'd be married in no time. To some safe, suburban local lad, and then Chloe told me that you wrote to each other.'

'Chloe!'

'Sure, I learned that you lived at the

same flat, went back to the same job and after Marion's death I vowed I'd contact you as soon as possible. Well of all the times to pick having the measles, Chloe certainly picked the wrong time.' He laughed at her amazed expression. 'Well she wasn't very well at all and we had a pretty worrying time of it; anyway, afterwards I came to see you. Nobody at home . . . so I cooled my heels at the local hotels for the night and next day rang your works and spoke to Anne.'

'And what had she to say to you?' she asked, amusedly.

'What did she not say to me . . . I met her for lunch and believe me, she wanted to know the whys and wherefores before she even breathed a hint of where you had gone. Still I think she's pretty reassured now of my intentions . . . er, honourable intentions.'

'So you knew I was here—' and then a sudden thought came to her. 'Jake,' she cried, 'do you think Chloe will take our marriage in her stride . . . and I wonder what Mrs Kennedy'll think about it all.'

'My dear girl, you should have seen them the day you sneaked off back to Durham. I was sent to Coventry for days . . . mind you I looked guilty and felt like hell, too. I got the big lecture off Rose Kennedy and tears and tantrums from my little daughter, too. Anyway I should think that they'll be highly delighted at the turn of events.'

The look she gave him was eloquent of her feelings and she noticed his grey eyes darken with longing at her. 'Don't you think we've wasted enough time talking?' he asked lowering his head slowly and tantalizingly towards her mouth. Melanie didn't hesitate, she too had waited long enough and threw her arms around his neck in response to the slow, lingering kiss.

'Melanie, Melanie, for God's sake . . .' She didn't give him time to finish his mild protest as she felt the trembling of his mouth as hers parted to succumb to the passion of his own. She heard him give a low groan as his kisses became wilder and felt the soft fur of the rug against her head as he lowered himself from the chair to lie across her, on the floor.

'Darling,' she breathed against his neck, wanting only to remain in quivering ectasy at his burning touch, her hands caressing the back of his neck as his mouth found the hollow between her breasts, her body arched soft and responsive against his hard masculinity.

'No, Melanie . . . ' he pleaded as he tried to raise his head but she only clutched him harder and brought her mouth into focus between his lips. 'You once asked me to love you . . . well I am . . . love me back, Jake . . . we've waited too long.'

The thin veil of perspiration on Jake's brow was indicative of the strain he was undergoing as he caught the hands round the back of his neck and withdrew them and clasped them against her sides on the floor. He ended their kiss and slowly, as in a daze, Melanie's eyes cleared slightly of the dark passion, glowing like green emeralds in her eyes.

'I need another drink,' was all he could say in a husky voice and got to his feet quickly leaving Melanie to relax like a contented kitten, snuggling against the softness of the rug.

'Melanie, for crying out loud . . . get up, before I take you here and now.'

She sighed and decided to obey the hoarse command, there would be plenty other times to share the delights of love.

★ ★ ★

Melanie nestled against the sweater-clad shoulder of her husband as the headlights of their car picked out the turn off for Beadnell.

'Soon be home, darling,' he murmured as she snuggled closer still.

'Hmm,' she sighed. 'Wish you were still lying on that beach, darling? It's a bit colder here.'

'I know where I'd like to be lying . . . just you wait till we get home.' He growled in an exaggerated manner as she laughed back at him.

His sensual manner had ceased to embarrass her, for they had now been married two months and she was used to his unexpected outbursts, and after the new realms of passionate ecstasy he had taught her to experience her shyness had soon disappeared, much to his delight.

Soon the house came into view as they turned in at the drive, all downstairs lights illuminating the welcome that they knew would be waiting them. She could discern the two figures of Rose Kennedy and Chloe waiting at the doorway; even now Chloe was waving her arms frantically at the car.

'You know . . . this place is just as nice as anywhere on the Bahamas . . . when you feel like we do together.'

'You were the one to choose the honeymoon . . . I'd have gone anywhere.'

'Oh, it was lovely, Jake . . . ' she protested at the thoughts of berating her idyllic surroundings in the Bahamas, 'but it's nice to come home.'

Kisses and hugs were in abundance as she slid out of the car; Chloe excitedly embracing one then the other; Rose, all smiles, beaming at the newly married pair. As they were preceded by them in the doorway, she felt a strong pair of arms sweep her from her feet and holding her against his chest he whispered, 'Can't disappoint them, darling,' and carried her over the threshold in the traditional manner, their love for each other showing plainly in their eyes for all to see.

'I'd like a new little brother first, daddy, then maybe a new sister . . . I haven't quite made up my mind yet,' demanded a small childish voice.

'I'll try and oblige,' was Jake's almost inaudible reply as he kissed his wife before setting her down on her feet.

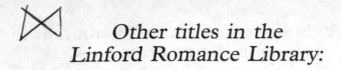

Other titles in the
Linford Romance Library:

NUDGING FATE

Marjorie Santer

After being widowed by a car accident Emma Dane decides to make a new life for herself and her young daughter, Jenny, back in the idyllic Norfolk countryside of her childhood. She finds a post teaching at the local school and although she quickly makes friends, the local vet seems determined to be rude and dismissive every time she sees him. Yet, despite his coldness, she can't seem to get him out of her mind . . .